MACLEAN

ALLAN DONALDSON

Vagrant Press is an imprint of
Nimbus Publishing Limited
PO Box 9166
Halifax, NS   B3K 5M8
(902) 455-4286

Printed and bound in Canada
Design: Aaron Harpell

Library and Archives Canada Cataloguing in Publication

    Donaldson, Allan
    Maclean / Allan Donaldson.
    ISBN 1-55109-550-5

I. Title.
PS8557.O51M33 2005   C813'.6   C2005-904388-1

We acknowledge the financial support of the Government of Canada through the Book Publishing Industry Development Program (BPIDP) and the Canada Council, and of the Province of Nova Scotia through the Department of Tourism, Culture and Heritage for our publishing activities.

To Marjory

1

He found himself labouring along a narrow, mud road, deeply pitted and rutted by the passage of great columns of men and wagons. On both sides, the road was fenced in by thick entanglements of barbed wire twisted and nailed every which-way to cross frames of rotting wood. Beyond the wire, bare, treeless fields stretched away into the distance, their emptiness broken here and there by the ruins of a house or the scattered remains of other entanglements. Some of the fields had once been ploughed, and long pools of stagnant water lay in the furrows, their surface swimming with green slime and small lumps of brown-gray stuff like drowned mice. A stink rose from the ground and drifted in waves across the road, so strong sometimes that he had trouble catching his breath.

The road ran straight and flat to the horizon, and at first it seemed to him that he was alone. Then he became aware that other soldiers had taken shape and were marching along with him. In the raw cold of the winter day, they were wearing great coats with the collars turned up close under their helmets, and they walked bent forward, their chins tucked down against their chests. He had the sense that they were men whom he knew, but although he leaned down to look up under the helmets, he couldn't make out their faces.

When he tried in an unreasoning terror of anxiety to speak to them, he found that he had lost his voice and could only make hoarse, inarticulate noises like those of a stricken animal.

Then abruptly the other soldiers were gone, and he was struggling through the mud as fast as he could because there was somewhere he had to get to before dark. Overhead, the sky was a uniform dirt-gray, and it began to rain, the kind of dead, straight rain that could go on all day and all night, relentless and unpitying, sometimes for weeks on end.

He began to run, but slowly, weighed down by his packs and the rifle which he now found himself to be carrying. After a few yards, he again became aware that he was not alone. A furlong behind, a man was following him, running, not fast but steadily, as if he could run forever. He had the sense that this too was someone whom he should recognize, but looking back over his shoulder, he could see the man's features only as a gray blur. Then the curtain of rain seemed to part, and he beheld, suddenly close up, the thin-lipped, skull-white face, the sunken, always searching, malevolent eyes.

His felt his bowels turning to water with fear.

It was Death. Sergeant Death.

Maclean awoke and stared up at the plaster ceiling. Like the sky in the dream which was sinking away from him even as he tried to recall it, the ceiling was dirt-gray except over the window, where a semi-circular, brown stain had been left behind by melt-water that had been dammed by ice on the eave of the house and had found its way back up under the shingles and down through the mouldering wood of the roof. This had happened over and over again, and the stain was crossed by a pattern of concentric lines, like contour lines on a map, each marking the limit of one of the water's successive advances. At the heart of the stain, over which all these advances had passed, the colour was as dark as the colour of encrusted blood. At the edge, it melted away into the gray nothingness of the unstained plaster.

He rolled over and looked at the room. The sun, still a summer sun, fell slantwise across the floor and part way up the wall opposite the bed. As the fall drew on, the band of light would narrow until it was hardly the width of a pencil; then, all through the dead of winter, it would grow again with the promise of spring. The wallpaper was decorated with alternating columns of red and yellow flowers, and he knew just where the light fell on those columns at every point in the cycle of the seasons. When he woke up and had got himself located, he could even tell to within a few minutes what time it was.

He had seen a sundial once, but it had been knocked over and the pedestal broken, lying in a yard littered with the wreckage of some rich family's life. Tiles, bricks, glass, mahogany sofas with the stuffing pouring out of the upholstery, splintered tables and chairs, smashed china, torn damask curtains, a shattered mirror in a gilded frame.

His room was hardly bigger than a cell. ("It gives people who ain't too steady on their feet sumpin' to hang onto so's they don't fall down and break their bones," Drusilla once said to him, giving him a heavy stare from under her brows.) It was also furnished hardly better than a cell. A dresser with a little mirror propped against the wall on top. A small table and two straight-backed chairs. A free-standing closet leaning against the wall on the uneven floor, doorless and crudely built out of some trashy wallboard that a man could have put his fist through without even skinning his knuckles. A slack-springed single bed.

None of this stuff belonged to him. In a quarter of an hour, he could have packed up everything he owned and departed the room, and the world, without a trace.

He picked up his watch from the table and held it up before his eyes. Twenty to seven. Saturday, August 21. It would be next Saturday at least before his cheque came, perhaps even the Monday or Tuesday after that. You could never tell with those people. Like most servants of the crown, they liked to let you know who was in charge by avoiding any unseemly show of haste. And it would be the Wednesday after that before any more of his liquor coupons came due. And tomorrow was his mother's birthday. 1870. 1943. Seventy-three. He had remembered it last Saturday, forgotten it, then remembered it again all of a sudden last night on the way home. He tried to calculate how much money he had brought back with him. Two dimes and a few pennies. And he still had a coupon left for a quart of wine. He would have to get some more money somehow.

He swung his legs down, sat on the edge of the bed, and became aware that although he hadn't drunk all that much the night before, his stomach felt queasy and there was a nasty taste at the back of his throat.

Outside, a slow, heavy tread went by his door and descended the stairs. It was followed almost at once by the quicker steps of two men coming along the hall together, talking about something to do with a motor car. Walter Haynes, the son of a whore, and the two MacDonald boys on their way to breakfast. From below, he heard the voice of Drusilla giving them orders about something or other.

He peeked out his door and saw that the bathroom was empty. Quickly, he put on an old plaid dressing gown, collected his shaving gear, and slipped across the hall.

He hadn't shaved yesterday, nor the day before, and the water from the tap wasn't any too hot, so he scraped away as cautiously as he could. When he had finished, he washed his face and hands and combed his hair. He was going to have to look like a man who could do some work, a man not on the booze, a man merely down on his luck a little through no fault of his own, a man deserving of a little consideration even in this inconsiderate world.

He studied himself in the mirror. Even shaved and combed, the man he saw was a creature he sometimes found it hard to identify with when he first confronted him in the morning—an angular scarecrow where once there had been a strong, not bad-looking man. At his peak, before the gas and the booze, he had weighed a hundred and eighty pounds, not an ounce of it fat. The last time he had weighed himself for a penny on a machine in Selrites, which also told his fortune (he was going on a long journey), he had weighed a hundred and forty-one. But Henry MacDade said that skinny people lived longer, and it was better to be a skinny pall-bearer than a fat corpse.

Back in his room, he got himself into his clothes. Wool socks, a heavy flannel shirt, heavy work trousers, work boots that weren't going to last much longer, an old suitcoat with leather patches on the elbows. When he had the coat on, he took a change purse out of the pocket and looked into it. There was only one dime, not two, and four pennies.

The hell with it. He would worry about it later. First, he needed some fresh air, then a good breakfast. Porridge, soft and bland, to soothe the stomach. With some brown sugar for energy. And a slice or two of bread and a couple of doughnuts.

He picked up his cap, went out, and carefully locked the door behind him. The big corner room next to his had been occupied for the last six months by Mrs. Fraser, an old woman, over eighty, who was dying slowly, getting whiter and thinner every week. She had been sent there to do her dying by two daughters who lived uptown and came down once or twice a month to see how it was going along. Sometimes as he went past her door, he spoke to her, but she was asleep now, lying on her back with her mouth open, tiny in the double bed like some scrimpy rag doll that God had made to stick pins into.

Quickly, quietly, he descended the stairs, met nobody, and went straight out into the morning sunlight pouring down over the hills on the far side of the river. Setting his cap on his head, giving it a final, resolute twist, he crossed the dirt road in front of the boarding house and made his way through a little field of sparse sword-grass and stunted weeds to the gravel shore above the rounded rocks of the riverbed.

Beside him, minnows darted in the pools among the rocks, and a long-legged shore bird, foraging, kept its distance thirty feet ahead. In the grass, a band of rubbish marked the furthest reach of the high water in the spring. He had passed it a hundred times before, but out of habit he cast his eyes over it as he walked. Driftwood polished smooth by the river. A broken board with a line of rusted nails. Rusted cans. Rags that must once have been clothes. Bottles filled with sand. Nothing salvageable. Nothing saleable. In a shallow pool among the rocks, a dead sucker lay with its bloated, green-white belly turned up out of the water.

A furlong from the house, he turned into a little patch of woods. The nearer trees were riverbank trash—alders, chokecherries, pople—but a little way back where the ground rose and became drier, there was a grove of maples and ancient oak and butternut trees that the squirrels liked.

One summer he had trained a gray squirrel to take food from his hand. He would sit on one end of a fallen trunk and click his tongue, and the squirrel would come down out of the tree where it had been waiting for him and sit on the other end of the trunk, upright, its paws held close together against its white chest. When he held out the peanut he had brought, it would come along the trunk in a succession of little rushes, stop, place one small, cool paw on his hand, pause to look up at him with its dark, impenetrable eyes, delicately take the peanut between its teeth, and scurry back to the other end of the trunk to eat it.

Then one morning, it didn't come, nor the next morning either, nor any morning again ever. Someone had shot it just for the hell of it, or a dog had killed it just for the hell of it, and he had never tried to tame another one to take its place. It crossed his mind that it might have been killed because he had wooed away too much of its instinctive distrust of mankind.

He walked up into the grove and slowed his pace. He liked the abrupt sense of seclusion, the broken, early-morning light slanting down through the trees, and the traffic of birds on their first rounds of the day—sparrows, chickadees, nuthatches, goldfinches, robins, bluejays, sometimes a great pileated woodpecker like some exotic migrant from a tropical island, sometimes one of the few bluebirds that had not yet vanished. There had once, he remembered, been bluebirds in every field, and when he was a boy, he and his sister Alice used to put up houses for them on fence posts.

He walked for a quarter of an hour before turning back. At the edge of the grove, he stopped and looked across the river at the steep hills with their farmhouses and barns perched among fields that were already yellowing towards autumn. Along the face of the hills, a flock of crows was flying in a ragged line upriver, labouring heavily the way crows do, as if God had never meant them to fly at all. And high in the pure air, above the line of crows and the top of the hills, the hawk who always fished there in the morning was circling, floating, without so much as the flick of a wing.

Mrs. Drusilla Ellsworthy stood in the door between the kitchen and the boarders' dining room, her hands on her hips, her expression commanding.

"You gotta git them there new ration books today," she repeated in slow, round tones as if addressing an assembly of half-wits. "You gotta fill out that there sheet at the back of the old book and you gotta leave it in the book and take the old book to them entire. You unnerstand? En-tire. This is the last day. You unnerstand? You gotta go to the town hall or the high school."

Drusilla had been born in a God-forsaken little settlement on the Moose Lake Road, and she had come to town with a view to bettering herself. Mr. Elsworthy—Mr. Elmer Elsworthy—was a pinch-faced, little Englishman with a runny nose who talked all the time as if he had a mouthful of sticky candy and pronounced "come" as "cum," "love" as "luv" and so on. He had come to Wakefield after the Great War with some money from somewhere, had caught the eye of the plump Drusilla, been taken to her ample bosom and permitted to make her his bride. With his money, they had bought this decaying house, fixed it up so it wouldn't, for another few years, fall down, and set up as boarding house keepers.

"The town hall or the high school," Drusilla intoned. "You unnerstand, Pinky? You gotta do it today."

"Yes," Maclean said. "I'll manage to get my mind around it somehow."

He was sitting in his accustomed place at the table in the boarders' dining room.

Walter Haynes, who worked at the pumping station, and the two MacDonald boys, who worked at a sawmill and who were expecting to be called up any day, had gone off to their jobs. Maclean was breakfasting as usual with Henry MacDade and Miss Audrey Sweet.

Henry, though only in his early fifties, was retired. After thirty years of unprofitable distress, he had decided that he didn't have whatever it took to be a successful farmer, so he had sold his farm, moved into town, and settled in Drusilla's boarding house. Miss Audrey Sweet, who did housework for the well-to-do, didn't go to work until nine when the well-to-do she worked for had finished breakfast.

"I got mine yesterday," Miss Audrey said. "I got mine at the town hall, and there was an awful lot of people."

"They should give people a whole week, not just a couple of days," Henry said.

"Well, they don't give no whole week," Drusilla said, "and there ain't nothin' I kin do about that. But I gotta git them coupons if you're gonna eat here."

And she went off to the kitchen.

Maclean looked down at his bowl of porridge. There had been no brown sugar and no maple sugar either, only corn syrup, which was sweet but tasteless. And there hadn't been any doughnuts either, only johnny cake.

"I could help you fill that form in, Mr. Maclean," Miss Audrey said. "I done mine, so's I know all about it."

"No," Maclean said. "Thanks. I can do it all right. It won't be any great trouble."

Miss Audrey Sweet, whom some of the town jokers called Sweet Audrey, was Maclean's age more or less. She had reddish-blonde hair, growing crinkly now and a little gray, and a round face set in an expression of perpetual concern lest something she could do to help might slip by undone. Her plump barrel of a body was mounted on short, plump legs, and even crossing a room, she gave an impression of furious activity as if she were struggling to walk fast up a steep bank.

When she was a young woman, sometime just after the Great War, she had had a baby which she had had no husband for and which had died after only a few weeks. A blessing, everyone said, but Miss Audrey hadn't thought so, and she had tried to kill herself by drinking something. Over the years, there had been much witty, sometimes blasphemous, speculation about who the father might be, but she never said, and no one ever knew. Now she was beginning to seem a little odd, maybe because of all that, maybe just because of her time of life.

She always addressed Maclean as "Mr. Maclean," and he wondered sometimes whether some of the sweet of Sweet Audrey might not be directed at him. He had even wondered once or twice late at night, when the rigid bonds of the daylight world had loosened a little, whether the two of them might not do worse than set up together.

There flickered momentarily into his mind the remembrance of a great wall of lighted windows, a courtyard with some kind of monument in the middle like a melted candle. Masses of people, soldiers, civilians, tremendous noise, talk, shouts, engines, a line of parked ambulances with red crosses on the sides and roofs. A faint mist of rain. And a girl in the shadows just inside the archway saying to him in a low voice as he went past towards the station, "A little comfort, soldier, before you go back over there?"

Seated in one of the wicker chairs on the front porch, Maclean rolled and lit his first cigarette of the day and began to cough.

"Everyone one of them cigarettes is another nail in your coffin," Henry MacDade said from the wicker chair next to him.

"There ain't room for any more nails in my coffin," Maclean said.

Every morning when Maclean lit his cigarette, Henry made this same remark about the nail. Every morning Maclean made the same reply, and every morning Henry laughed and slapped his thigh as if it were all being said for the first time.

Henry was a plump little man, always smiling, always

talkative. He was interested in history, geography, and science. He had a card to the library and a small brass telescope that he used to take out to the riverbank sometimes at night, where he would sit for hours on a big rock with a book and a flashlight keeping tabs on the goings-on in the heavens.

"Did you know that Napoleon Buonaparte was an Eyetalian?" he said to Maclean.

"No," Maclean lied. "No, I didn't."

"That's right," Henry said. "Not a Frenchman at all. An Eyetalian."

"Well, well," Maclean said.

He was trying to think through his day, and right now he didn't have time for Napoleon no matter where he came from, but he didn't want to hurt Henry's feelings. Henry was a simple, good-hearted soul who often gave him liquor coupons at the first of the month. He didn't drink and had no need of them himself, but he could have sold them for a quarter or two at the first of the month and for just about anything to some people at the end.

"Eyetalian," Henry said. "Born in Corsica, which is an Eyetalian island in the Mediterranean Sea."

"Well, well," Maclean said.

He was going to need a dollar at least, maybe a dollar and a half. A bottle of wine for himself and a birthday present for his mother. He might pick up some beer bottles, but they wouldn't amount to much. He was going to have to get a couple of hours' work somewhere, maybe at Jim Gartley's stable. Then before dinner go to the high school and get the god-damned ration book.

From the door beside them, Miss Audrey came out with her big handbag full of cleaning stuff. She lowered herself sideways down the steps and set off up the road towards town, her big bottom rolling, her fat little legs pumping away but making such slow headway that you could imagine that the road beneath her feet was a conveyer belt carrying her backward half as fast as she walked.

Maclean watched her out of sight, and before Henry could get back to Napoleon, said he had to be on his way too and got up and followed.

2

The railroad bridge at the mouth of the creek that ran through the middle of town was three spans across—a centre span with low steel trusses at the sides and two, shorter spans at either end with nothing at their sides but the forty-foot drop down to the rocky creek bed. A couple of hundred yards upstream there was a street bridge, but Maclean didn't have time this morning to walk an extra quarter-mile for nothing.

He knew the times of the passenger trains well enough. It was the freights that were dangerous. He stood at the end of the bridge and listened, then got down and put his ear to the rail. Nothing. Stepping carefully on every other tie, trying not to look down between them at the the water foaming and eddying among the rocks, he made his way to the centre span. He leaned against one of the trusses, listened again, heard nothing, and, footing it as fast as he dared, went on across the last span.

"I seen you, Mr. Maclean, walking on that railroad bridge again," Miss Audrey said. "I was on the town bridge, where you should'a been, and I seen you. That railroad bridge ain't no place for a man your age."

Off the end of the bridge, a line of decaying coal sheds

ran beside an abandoned siding. He slowed down to scout for beer bottles, but there was nothing, only a skinny cat that started and fled away into the weeds. Another minute brought him into town beside the General Store, a great, three-storey barn of a building with another trail of sheds along the railway.

A cluster of men in from the country had already gathered in front of the store. Even at a distance he could hear the nasal, know-it-all voices whining about the things they always whined about: the weather, the high price of feed, the low price of potatoes, school taxes, road taxes, the government.

As he passed, he sensed their eyes following him out of sight, and he was so taken up with his black hatred of them that he almost walked right past. Three quart Moosehead bottles, standing neatly in a row against the shed wall, as if left there for him. Some soldiers had stood them there the night before maybe because they couldn't be bothered with them. Or maybe somebody in the feed shed was drinking on the sly. Or maybe the Almighty and Most Merciful Father, who sees the little sparrow fall, had decided this morning in his whimsical and unfathomable way to dish him up a little mercy for a change.

He cashed the bottles in at a place that bought empty bottles—and under the counter sold a few full ones as well—and came out with twelve cents. With the fourteen he had brought with him, he was already up to twenty-six. He began to think it was going to be a good day.

Jim Gartley's stable was on Diamond Street, which was more an alley than a street and was certainly no jewel—a kind of wooden canyon whose walls were made up mostly of the sides and backs of buildings that faced on other streets.

Before the Great War, before Henry Ford and the god-damned motor car, Gartley's stable had been a good business. Now it housed in any regular way only a few delivery horses and a few horses belonging to old men who hated the motor car and still drove around town in buggies. Seeing the way the wind was blowing, Jim had set up a gas pump out front and had started garaging cars for people who put them up in the winter.

The big double doors were wide open, and Maclean walked in, not hurrying, ambling, wanting to feel things out before he tried to see about a little work. There were half a dozen horses in the stalls, but no sign of anyone around. He didn't want to knock on the office door for fear of interrupting something important, so he walked down along the line of stalls past the great rumps of the horses. Work horses snuffling and moving their feet around, staring at the wooden wall above the bins in front of them. (What did they think about there, each one alone, all day and all night?)

At the back of the stable was a little workshop. Maclean peeked around the corner of the door. Sam Kelly was sitting astradle a saw horse working on a piece of harness with a leather punch. He didn't hear Maclean. He was sixty and a little deaf. He was also a little simple, but he was a good man with horses, and he had worked in the stable almost all his life. Jim's father, old Nate, had hired him. Old Nate had been killed, kicked by a horse one day for no reason at all, straight into the guts so that he died right there on the stable floor just as if he'd been shot.

The shells came out of nowhere all together. No one heard them because of all the noise on the road—wagons rattling, truck motors roaring, people shouting, cursing. A whole battery must have loaded up and fired all at once, and they must have had the road zeroed in beforehand. The shells landed on both sides so fast that they seemed like one, long, continuous explosion. If the ground had been mud, it would have been bad enough, but it was stone and hard clay, and there was metal flying everywhere. A dozen or more killed on the spot, a lot more wounded. One shell landed beside a wagon and blew it to pieces and killed all the men on it and one of the horses. The other went careening, staggering, half-sideways off the road, screaming like a banshee, trailing harness and half of a broken whiffle-tree and a stream of guts and blood that poured out of its belly. It went fifty yards or more before it finally fell over and died. Afterwards, further up the road, they came to another place where a dozen horses, some still harnessed together, were lying beside the road, bloated, their legs sticking straight out like poles, teeming with flies, blue with them.

Maclean tapped on the door, and Sam looked up. He was short, fat, and bow-legged.

"Hello, Pinky," he said. "How ya been doin'?"

"Good," Maclean said. "The very best."

Sam looked at him over his shoulder, a look that Maclean knew very well, a look that was asking itself how much he might have had to drink already this morning.

"Business good?" Maclean asked. "See you got a few horses in there."

"Not bad," Sam said.

Maclean waited for Sam to perhaps give him a lead in, but Sam just went on tapping at the harness.

"Don't suppose Jim has any little chores he might want done?" Maclean asked finally.

"Couldn't say," Sam said. "He ain't said nothin' to me. You don't know nothin' about fixin' harness, I don't suppose?"

Sam could be a son of a whore when he set his mind to it.

"Well, perhaps I better ask him," Maclean said.

"He ain't in," Sam said. "He went downtown to fetch sumpin'."

"He going to be long, you think?"

"I don't know," Sam said. "He might git talkin'. You never know."

"No," Maclean said. "That's it."

He left Sam and walked back down through the twilight of the stable past the great rumps of the work horses and the idly switching tails. He stood in the doorway and looked up and down the street. There was no sign of Jim, but at the corner of Main Street, four of the boys were hanging around talking. If they saw him, they would guess that he might be into the money, and if they came down and Jim found them there, they would screw up everything.

He sat down on a wooden bench just inside the door where he could get the sun that was beginning to angle in above the roofs down the street. Left alone, suspended, he began to think he would like a drink.

He didn't notice Jim until he was already at the door.

"Hello, John," Jim said. "Ain't seen you in a while. How've you been?"

He looked at Maclean the way Sam Kelly had earlier, his eyes posing the same question.

Jim Gartley was six foot with dark hair and a neat, dark moustache. Even when he was at the stable, he was something of a dude, in a flashy, light tweed suit and a shirt and tie and polished, black, pointed shoes. He was a second cousin to Maclean, and he used to be around their house sometimes when he was a boy before the Great War.

"Fine," Maclean said. "Just fine."

"And your mother? How is she?"

"Fine. Not any worse anyways," he said and began edging out onto the ice. "The thing is, tomorrow's her birthday, and it's getting near the end of the month, so I'm a little short. I wanted to get her a little something for a present, you know. And I was wondering if maybe you might have some chores around I could give you a hand with."

Maclean and Jim both knew, and knew that the other knew, that this business of chores was just a pretense. If there had been chores to do, Sam Kelly wouldn't have been sitting around pounding holes in a piece of leather.

Jim looked down the stable. Maclean never worked this oftener than once every three or four months, and Jim had never refused him.

"Well," he said, "it might not hurt to give some of them horses a bit of a rub. And a couple of handfuls of oats. And maybe clean up a little. I can give you a couple of hours, but I don't really need no more than that."

"That'll be great," Maclean said. "That'll suit me perfect."

"You know where the stuff is."

"Yes," Maclean said. "I know where everything is. Don't you bother about that."

Maclean began with a mare with a white blaze on her forehead that he had groomed before, working down her neck and shoulder with the currycomb while she stood lifting her head a little like a cat that is being petted, now and then snuffling and shivering her hide under the brush. When he had finished one shoulder, he got some oats and let her eat them out of his hand while he began working down the other shoulder.

Maclean didn't hear him until a board creaked under his foot as he crept the last step and his hand fastened on the back of Maclean's shirt and pulled it tight against his throat, hauling him up until only his toes touched the floor. Then the harsh voice that always sounded as if he had something stuck in his throat.

"You little sneak. I'll teach you to do as you're told, or I'll strip the hide off your back."

A blow to the side of his head with the free hand, then pushed, stumbling, half-falling and being hauled back onto his feet again, out into the hot sunlight of the yard and the heavy alder switch across his back and crouching there afterwards on his hands and knees crying as the heavy boots strode back into the barn. Then the sound of the switch against Nellie's haunches and the neighing and the hoofs pawing uselessly around in the stall.

He was sitting wedged into a little corner between the chicken house and a cedar rail fence. That was where Alice, always the protective elder sister, found him.

"What did you do?" she asked, kneeling in front of him.

"I gave Nellie some of the oats in the barn, and he'd told me not to."

"You should have asked first," Alice said.

"I didn't think a few like that were going to matter."

"Well," she said, "don't cry any more. It's over now. I brought you a cookie."

"I want to go far away and never come back."

"If I let him do things when I've told him not to, he'll grow up to be no good."

He was eating bread and milk while the others ate pancakes.

"Well, yes," his mother said. "I suppose that's true."

"Spare the rod and spoil the child."

He sat at the head of the table, a short man with a square head, close-cropped hair, heavy brows, and lips so thin he seemed hardly to have any lips at all.

He never smiled. Before every meal, he thanked God for giving them something to eat and prayed that the people in his care would walk in God's ways.

"Did ya hear the McIntyre boy got killed. Him that used to box, remember?"

Sam Kelly stood leaning, bow-legged, against the corner of the stall.

"No," Maclean said. "No, I didn't hear that. That's too bad."

"Somewhere's in Italy or someplace like that. He was in the Carleton-Yorks. They got a letter about it. It said he didn't suffer
no pain."

"That's good anyways," Maclean said. "That's good for his mother to know. Even if it ain't true."

The letters always said that. He had seen one of them

after he came back. Old Mrs. Simpson got him to come and see her, and she had the letter, all ragged from having been read so many times. She started crying again as soon as she looked at it. And yes, he had said, that was right, all right. He hadn't suffered any pain at all. He hadn't seen it happen himself, but he had heard all about it from some of the other boys.

And what he had heard was that Charlie had got shot in the belly and lay out between the lines all morning, working off in a few hours whatever years in hell might have been his due. Then he got carried in and lay outside a dressing station for another two hours before he died because there was nothing they could do for him anyway.

"His picture's gonna be in the paper next week," Sam said.

"That's good," Maclean said.

He finished the horse and stood back to look at her. He had worked hard on her, too hard, and he was out of breath. The dust and stuff in the stable always did that anyway. He put the currycomb on the edge of the stall and walked out to the door of the stable, leaned against the jamb, rolled a cigarette, lit it, and began to cough.

"I pay Sam forty cents," Jim said, "so I got to pay you a little less, so he don't feel bad."

This was the way they always did it.

"Sure, absolutely," Maclean said. "That's only fair."

"So," Jim said, "you were a couple of hours and little over, so let's say seventy-five cents."

He gave Maclean a fifty-cent piece and a quarter.

"But I'd like to see that Aunt Hilda got something nice for

her birthday, so here's another fifty cents for that. That ain't pay, you understand."

"No, no," Maclean said. "I understand. And I won't say a word to Sam or anyone else. Except mother. I'll tell her you helped me out."

"You tell her happy birthday from Nancy and me," Jim said.

Maclean looked at the three coins lying in his palm. This was far more than he had ever hoped to come by.

"I wouldn't want Aunt Hilda not to get something," Jim was saying, his head cocked a little to one side, watching Maclean, silently telling him, "I don't want you to go off and drink this all up."

"She'll get something nice," Maclean said. "Don't you worry about that. And I'll tell her you and Nancy were asking after her. And about the work and the money and all."

At the stable door, he looked towards Main Street. He didn't see any of the boys there now, but they could have been just around the corner, so he cut into a little alley and came out further up Main Street beside the post office. He took a quick look around. There was no one down Main Street, no one at the corner, no one in front of the liquor store. Someone had come up with a bottle, and they had gone off. Or the cops had run them off.

The street was lined on both sides with cars and trucks, and the Saturday crowds on the sidewalks were thickening up. Across the street in front of the town hall, people were lined up to get the new ration books, but the police station and the lockup were also in the town hall, and Maclean had decided to get his ration book at the high school. He hadn't done anything to get himself in trouble, but the less the cops saw of you the better.

He made his way across Main Street through the crawling traffic, half-expecting someone to shout after him. Someone who had seen him around the stable. Someone who would know he was in the money.

Up the street, walking fast, getting a little winded, he passed the Court House and looked as he always did at the cenotaph and the old German field gun which stood on either side of the lawn out front. It was the only German gun he had ever seen. They were always going to get the bastards who were shelling them, but they never did.

The cenotaph was a thick, square column of black granite with a soldier on top standing at attention with his rifle at his side. The sides of the column were covered with tablets listing the dead, and as Maclean passed, names leapt out at him. Robert Cronk. Charles Simpson. Frank Gallagher. Old pals whose faces he sometimes had a hard time remembering now, especially when he was sober, although sometimes when he was drinking, one or the other of them would suddenly without warning take shape so clear he could imagine him speaking.

Hello, Johnnie, I hardly knew ya.

Where had it been? France somewhere. A summer day well away from the trenches on their way to an inspection by General somebody or other. A long column of them, a mile or more, with a band somewhere in the middle. It was playing The Soldiers of the King, and they were expected to sing along to show they were in good spirits. Most of them had been taught the words in school except that then it had been The Soldiers of the Queen. All the little boys marching around the room and the girls sitting at their desks waving as if they were saying goodbye to them as they set off to the war. The Boer War that would have been. And Miss Thatcher, a tight-limbed, fierce little woman standing up in front of the blackboard beating out the time with a ruler.

"We're the soldiers of the Queen, my lads."

He remembered the day the old Queen died. A bitter, cold, winter day. From across the river, they heard all the bells on the hills of the town tolling, and people came out and stood along the banks of snow by the road looking across the ice, thinking there must be a fire. Then someone coming from town told them that the Queen had died, and his mother and Alice started crying and wiping their eyes, standing there on the road in the cold, and some of the men took off their hats. Crazy. And he remembered, it must have been the next Saturday, all the buildings on Main Street draped in black and the snow falling and the dung from the horses steaming in the streets.

3

The new high school was a great brick building with ten-foot-high, arched windows on the second floor, a gift to the town by its only millionaire, a monument to the dignity of learning. When Maclean had gone to high school, the building had been wooden with a big steeple up the centre like a church and two wings running off to the sides with little roofed walkways along the front behind a line of arches, like the ones he had seen the time he and two of the boys had gone to Westminster Abbey. A little square of grass and around it, the walkway with the arches and a square of blue sky overhead, all just as it must have been five hundred years before so that you could imagine that you really had stepped back into that quiet time.

But as they were walking around, three big, awkward farmboys, gawking and marveling in their farmboy way, an English captain had shouted at them, "You men. You men there. What business have you here? Get out where you belong. This isn't Piccadilly Circus. This isn't a public house."

And they had all saluted and snuck out like children.

Maclean entered the school past a sign about the ration books, which he didn't bother to read, and climbed the stairs into the central hall. A couple of trestle tables had been set up at one end, and a line of fifty people or more, mostly women, were trailing back from them. He tacked onto the end of the line behind a fat woman in a silk dress, who looked at him as if she might be getting ready to throw up and stepped up beside the woman in front of her.

Maclean left her three feet of breathing room and stood gazing around, detaching himself. The walls of the hall were lined with pictures of graduating classes. His mother would be there somewhere. And Miss Audrey Sweet, who had graduated before her calamity plunged her back into the great slough from which she had managed briefly to clamber. He himself was in none of them, though somewhere there would be one that a ghost of him might be in, waiting to step out, as the group dissolved, into the ghost of the life he had never had.

Latin and Mathematics are a training for the mind.

He hadn't known that day when he left school for home that it would be his last day.

"What does he need a high school diploma for?" his father shouted at his mother. "The horses can't read. Neither can the pigs. Maybe he can recite Latin to them. Or Shakespeare."

Amo, amas, amat. This blessed plot, this earth, this realm, this England. Neco, necas, necat. Necavi, necavisti, necavit. Necaverunt. For -erunt, -ere is also found, especially in poetry.

The worst thing was going back to get the stuff from his desk. It was early in March. Overnight the temperature had gone up into the forties. There was water melting and running everywhere, and the light falling now from a different place in the sky seemed all of a sudden in that warm air no longer the hard light of winter.

He went over around four o'clock when the others would have been gone. But they weren't all gone, and three of the boys in his grade were standing in the hall. And Cynthia. That was the worst of all. They watched him and didn't speak. He could tell they had some sense of what was going on. Maybe the word had trickled back somehow from across the river. Maybe they had merely guessed at it because of the days he had already missed, he who was never sick and who never missed days. They were waiting maybe for him to speak, but he was ashamed as if somehow all along he had been in a place where he didn't belong and had now been exposed for the imposter he was.

Standing, shunned, behind the fat lady in her silk dress, looking at the long rows of graduation photographs, he could feel it all again. One of the boys once told him a story about a vacant house that had been hit by lightning. The people had moved out, too hurried or too lazy to take the bulbs out of the sockets, but the power had been cut off, so the wires inside were all dead. Then one night, the chimney had been hit by lightning, and for a few seconds all the lights in the house had come on. It was like that. There were all these hidden people there inside him, all those slumbering ghosts, like dark houses with dead wires, and every once in a while something would come like the lightning bolt, and all the dead circuitry of their grief would come to life.

The principal of the school was Mr. Raymond from one of the old Anglican families in the town. Tall with long, wild hair and wide, dark eyes. The girls adored him. He taught English composition, English literature, and Latin, and he was fond of declaiming poetry. Catullus, Shakespeare, Wordsworth, Keats, Tennyson. And Yeats and Carman, both of whom he had met. Carman was a distant relative, and Mr. Raymond promised that when next he saw Carman, he would try to persuade him to come and read to them.

Past the lighthouse, past the nunbuoy,
Past the crimson, rising sun,
There are dreams go down the harbour
With the tall ships of Saint John.

Mr. Raymond was sitting behind the desk in his class-room. He too had probably guessed what had happened.

"They need me at home," Maclean said, offhand, swaggering, trying to make as if he were saying, "I'm a man now, and I haven't time for all this."

"That's too bad," Mr. Raymond said. "You were doing well. Perhaps you'll be able to come back next year. You could work at some of the books."

"I'll see," Maclean said.

He got his things out of the desk, not looking up, and stuffed them roughly into the bookbag. He was determined never to look at them again.

"I'm sorry to see you go," Mr. Raymond said. "And I want to wish you good luck whatever you do."

As it turned out, he was the one who was going to need the luck, more of it than he had anyway. Three years later

he was dead. Like almost all the young men from those old
families with their worship of England, he joined up and
became an officer, and one day a great German shell came
down on the arm of their trench and blew him and everyone else to pieces so small that one of the boys told him
later there was hardly anything left to bury. After the war,
somebody published a little book of poems he had written,
all about birds and flowers. Crazy.

Atque in perpetuum, frater, ave atque vale

The town clock on the top of the post office was striking
twelve as he hustled back, straight down Main Street and
to hell with it. God damn them. The miserable, little fuckers. Is this your ration book? Yes, it's my book, it's got my
name in it. Yes, but that doesn't mean you're the person that's
got the name that's in the book. We have orders to be sure.
Jesus Christ, you've seen me a thousand times. You know
god-damned well who I am. What the hell are you talking
about?

Now he was going to be late for his god-damned dinner.

"Pinky," someone shouted from behind him.

He looked back over his shoulder without stopping. It was
Junior Tedley, one of the boys he had seen hanging around
the end of Diamond Street. A bum. A leech. A useless,
splay-footed, chicken-brained, sponging son of a whore.

"Fuck off," Maclean said.

Drusilla was a little behind with dinner, and she was still
dishing up the Saturday beef stew when Maclean slipped
into his place. The boarders sat down the sides of the table,

and there was an empty space at the end where Mr. Elmer Ellsworthy sometimes ate his dinner when something interesting was being talked about.

What was interesting today was that the MacDonald boys had stopped at the post office on the way home, and Alex, the older one, had found his call-up notice waiting.

"You gonna volunteer for overseas?" Walter Haynes asked.

"I dunno," Alex said. "I ain't thought about it yet."

"You know all about that, Mr. Maclean," Miss Audrey said.

"About what would that be?" Maclean asked.

"Yes, sir," Henry said. "You been through it all. Vimy Ridge and all."

"I wasn't at Vimy Ridge," Maclean said.

"A lot of them guys," Walter said, "talk about the war that never got near no trenches. They just set around England not doin' nothin'."

"Well, you never seen no trenches anyway," Maclean said and immediately regretted it. Walter was a mean, underhanded son of a bitch, and it made no sense to get on the bad side of him over nothing.

He looked across at Maclean as if wondering which part of him he was going to hit first. Walter was bald with a fat, pink face and very small eyes set too close together. Altogether he looked like a pig except that the expression on a pig's face was generally more intelligent.

"I had a bad heart," Walter said. "I kept goin' down there to the Armoury, and they kept tellin' me, 'Walter you got a bad heart. With a heart like that, Walter, it would kill you in a week. With a heart like that, it's just a wonder you're alive.'"

"It's a great honour to serve one's King and Coontry," Elmer pronounced from the end of the table. "The greatest honour there is."

"Ours not to reason why," he intoned with upturned eyes. "Ours but to do and die. That's what Mr. Churchill says."

"Bullshit," Maclean said into his plate.

"Now, Mr. Maclean," Miss Audrey said, "I didn't hear that."

Maclean sat beside Henry on the front porch smoking a cigarette. The temperature had climbed all morning, and it was now nearly eighty, one of the last of the real summer days. Across the river, on the road that slanted up the face of the hill, a wagon loaded with bales of hay was being hauled up by a two-horse team so slowly that it seemed hardly to be moving.

"Did you know," Henry said, "that them stars we look at ain't really there like that any more? What we're looking at is the light they gave off thousands of years ago, so when we look at them, we're looking back all that time."

"Well, well," Maclean said.

"I read somewhere in a book," Henry said, "that there's some philosopher who says that all the time that ever was is still right here, only in a different place. Now ain't that something interesting to think about?"

"It is so," Maclean said.

With a hearty dinner in it, his stomach was feeling good now, and with all his worries cleared away, and the where-withal in his pocket, he was feeling the need for a drink, a need all its own, like hunger or thirst or the need for a cigarette, but with its own peculiar quality of need the way each of those things had its own peculiar quality. It was a kind of void located at first somewhere at the back of the throat, then radiating out, spreading further and further as time went on, the way the good first drink radiated out, chasing that void and transforming it into lightness and a joy that passeth understanding.

If it hadn't been for all the time he had wasted at the high school, he would have had time to stop at the liquor store and get something before dinner.

But it would have been crazy to stop when he had all that money on him. And if he'd got drinking, he could have ended up getting himself rolled somewhere. Better to do what he had done.

He would leave some of the money here and then go up town. But first he would have a nap. The work, the brisk walk to the school, the standing around, the half-run back here had tired him out. He could hang on for another hour, then everything would be set up fine, and he would be feeling rested and ready.

The dresser in his room had two small drawers at the top with a space under them big enough that something not too thick could be put there and the drawer run back in. This was where he hid money and ration coupons when he had more than he wanted to carry. His door had a lock, but Drusilla kept a key so that she and her two fat daughters could come in to clean up, and anyway the lock was so crude that anybody who took the trouble could open it with a piece of baling wire.

Maclean put the ration book with his new liquor coupons and a fifty-cent piece and a quarter into an envelope and slipped them into his hiding place. Then he drew down the blind against the sunlight, took off his boots, and lay down. He looked at the stain on the ceiling and felt the memory of something he didn't want to remember beginning to stir. He put it away and thought instead of the good afternoon that awaited him on the far side of his sleep.

4

His legs rested up, his wind back, his dinner well settled, feeling good, Maclean strolled off the little, one-span bridge across the creek and into the square at the foot of Main Street, having taken the long, safe route uptown instead of the short, dangerous one, not in any hurry now, the assurance of the coins in his pocket making his thirst a feeling not of desperate anxiety, but of pleasant anticipation.

The square was at its fullest. Everyone was in town by now who was going to be there, and no one was setting off yet for even the longest drive home. Every parking space around the edge of the square and down the middle was taken up with cars, trucks, and wagons. The sidewalks packed with people, walking fast with somewhere to go, walking easy with nowhere particular to go, just standing, talking, watching the familiar turns of the weekly circus.

Maclean walked along the bottom of the square and made his way uptown through the crowd, catching snatches of talk out of the general uproar. "I never seen a summer like it. Somebody said it's all that stuff that's blowin' up in Europe...Now them there cows, I just don't see how they got across that river...By Jesus, boys, you should of seen that old dog run...Now his wife was a second cousin once removed...Now what that there god-damned government should do…" Talk that stopped sometimes in mid-sentence, trailing off as he went past, picking up sometimes when he was not quite far enough away not to hear. "John Maclean…You remember old Angus that farmed across the river…war…drink…something terrible."

Once, younger, bigger, stronger, and stupider, he had turned around and knocked a man off the sidewalk and down onto the street between a couple of parked cars and got himself a week in jail. The disgrace, Alice said. Mother, Alice said. What are you doing to yourself? Alice said.

Out of the square on his way up Main Street, he checked the side-streets and alleys for somebody good to get together with. Drinking by yourself was bad—bad for the head because you drank too fast, and dangerous if anything happened, if you choked, or had an attack, or got ganged up on by some guys who wanted somebody to beat up just for the hell of it.

Around the corner of the first alley he went by, there was a sagging wooden staircase that the boys sometimes drank under, but there was nobody there, and no one in the little alley by the Carleton Hotel, nobody on the corner of Diamond Street or anywhere along it, no one in front of the liquor store. He slowed down long enough to look inside as he went past. Some soldiers. Some rough characters from somewhere out in the woods. And standing at the counter, Mr. Magistrate Thurcott, very proper even on a hot afternoon like this in a trim, dark suit, just as if he was in court, buying his bottle of expensive sherry for a gentlemanly sip tomorrow between church and dinner. A wisp of nostalgia swept across Maclean's mind, as ephemeral as a puff of cigarette smoke in the wind. Almighty and most merciful Father.

Maclean went on up to the intersection at the top of Main Street that was the real centre of the town—fire station, town hall, library, and, most impressive and important of all, the post office, a three-storey mass of brick rising like a small mountain, sloping inwards and up to the great four-faced clock that you could see and hear even on the far side of the river.

Above the post office, a low granite wall separated the delivery way from the manicured lawn of the Anglican Church, and sitting on it, soaking up the sunshine, were Leveret Hershey and Ginger Coile. There were people Maclean would sooner have drunk with, but Leveret and Ginger would do if they had the money to pay their way.

Leveret Hershey, whom some of boys behind his back called "The Major" after Major Hoople in the comic strip, was a large man with a full paunch, a full head of gray hair, and a slow considered way of talking even when sober. He dressed himself in a succession of suits which he got from the Salvation Army, and he always wore a felt hat. For a while, he and Maclean had been together in the old Third Brigade that had been gloriously gassed and machine-gunned at Ypres, Festubert, and Givenchy, where Leveret lost the first three fingers off his left hand. He never knew how. One second they were there, he said, and the next second they were gone. And since you can't very well shoot a rifle, or even dig a ditch, with three fingers shot off, he was sent home. A small price to pay for getting out of there alive. By way of further compensation, he was given a small pension. Then a few years after he got home, he came into some money when his father died, and he hadn't worked a day since.

Ginger was young enough to have missed the Great War and just old enough not to have been called up for this one, not yet anyway, not until they got desperate for anybody who could stop a bullet or two, the way they had in 1917. He was a big man too, but, unlike Leveret, he didn't look like any major. He had tousled, red hair, none of his clothes seem to hang on him right, and he walked with a loose-limbed shamble, like an old dog. He was one of the strongest men in town. Maclean had once seen him on a bet lift a stove and carry it across the street. But whoever had put him together had run out of material before he got to the head and had left him a little simple. This was maybe why he was so attached to Leveret, whose brainless pomposities seemed to Ginger, even when he couldn't understand them, wisdom such as few ordinary mortals are privileged to hear. And for this privilege he was always ready to help Leveret out with a little of the cash he earned working at the jobs people thought him fit for, like wheeling cement or heaving barrels of potatoes onto a truck or carrying stoves across the street.

"Well, boys," Maclean said, as he ambled up to them, "this ain't a bad crack at a nice day."

"No," Leveret said. "I don't look for no snow, not before tomorrow anyways."

"So," Maclean asked, "what are you boys doing to put in the afternoon?"

"Nothin' special," Leveret said. "Nothin' special."

He shifted uneasily on the wall, lifting one buttock and setting it down again carefully a different way. Maclean sensed that something was up that Leveret was worried he might be an impediment to, no doubt through a lack of wherewithal.

But before he was too quick to let them know he wasn't on the bum, he decided he'd better wait and find out what was up and who might finish bumming from whom. Leveret, he knew from long experience, could be shifty.

On the sidewalk, Magistrate Thurcott went past carrying a little brown paper bag with his bottle of sherry, mincing along the way he did. His eyes flickered towards them and turned quickly away again. Theirs did the same, and he went on, up past the Anglican Church, where tomorrow he would sit and kneel and stand and sit down again and nod his head at the mention of the Lord's name. We have erred and strayed from thy ways like lost sheep.

"Pinky," he said, looking down, wearily, from the bench. "John. Mr. Maclean. You are a man of some education. What are you doing here?"

They watched him pass on up the street, and the silence spun itself out. Then Maclean became aware that Leveret wasn't looking at him any more but at something behind him and was nervously shifting his ass around again on the granite wall. Maclean turned and saw Jimmy McIninch and Bill Kayton coming around the corner of the post office.

Jimmy McIninch was a little Irish Catholic, but the practice of his Catholicism had long since lapsed although it was still touchy to say anything against Catholics or the church unless he said it himself first. He was five feet tall and weighed maybe a hundred and ten pounds. When he walked, he always looked as if he were sidling through a half-opened door, and the more worried or nervous he was the more he sidled. He was sidling now, and shrugging his shoulders, studying Maclean warily from under the peak of his cloth cap.

Bill Kayton was young enough to have been conscripted if it weren't for the drink. He was a wonderful carpenter when he was sober, and he could always get work since carpenters of any kind were scarce because of the war. People who hired him just took it for granted that every now and then he wouldn't be there in the morning, the way they took it for granted that every now and then they were going to lose a day or two because of the weather.

So Bill Kayton almost always had money, and as soon as Maclean saw him with Jimmy and saw Leveret dancing his ass around on the granite wall, he knew what was up. Leveret and the others had coupons but no money, and Bill Kayton would have money but no coupons, and Leveret was worried that he had arrived to join the party with neither one.

Jimmy and Bill came up, Jimmy sidling and shrugging like a monkey with fleas.

"A nice day," Maclean said.

"The very best," Bill said. "How you been?"

He acted as if he might already have had a drink or two, but drunk or sober, Bill was someone Maclean had always liked.

"Good," Maclean said. "Good. You ain't working today?"

"Never work on a Saturday," Bill said. "Five days shalt thou labour and on two shalt thou enjoy the fruits of thy labour."

The talk faltered, and they all stood around looking at each other.

"Well," Leveret said finally, when he saw that Maclean wasn't going to go away, "we were sort of wonderin' the four of us here, if we might not get together and get a little somethin' to drink."

"You got coupons," Bill said. "And I got a few dollars."

"Yes," Leveret said uneasily, eyeing Maclean. "Well, yes."

"Three coupons for wine, Jimmy told me," Bill said.

Maclean liked watching Leveret squirm, but he decided he had let it go on long enough.

"That's all right then," he said. "I'm fixed not too bad. I got a coupon and a little money, and I wouldn't mind coming in if that's all right."

"Well," Leveret said, brightening up. "We thought three bottles of port. Three bottles would make two dollars eighty-five."

He looked at Bill Kayton.

"Jimmy said you needed another dollar and a quarter."

"If that seems fair to you," Leveret said. "As a sort of trade for the coupons."

"Fair enough," Bill said.

"Well," Maclean said. "I got my coupon, so why don't we get four bottles. How would that be? And I could put in another sixty cents and just leave myself a little for some tobacco."

He looked at Bill Kayton.

"You couldn't manage another thirty-five cents?"

"Sure," Bill said.

"Well, then, boys," Leveret said, raising one arm expansively, to the alarm of a little old woman hustling past on the sidewalk. "There ain't gonna be many more days like this, so what do you say to the Black Rock?"

5

Half a mile up the tracks from the railroad bridge Maclean had crossed that morning, the Black Rock jutted out from the steep bank of the river. Twenty feet high, thirty feet long, shaped like the prow of a great ship, it was said to be part of the seam of an ancient volcano that the glaciers, the river, and the weather had disinterred and sculpted. At the end of a dry summer, the water at its base was hardly a foot deep, but in the spring freshet, the river, filled with floating ice cakes, rose half way up its sides, and then it did indeed seem like a great ship adrift in a hard-running winter sea.

From the railroad tracks, a steep path angled down to the rock through a jungle of chokecherry bushes. Below the bushes, the soil that had washed down the bank over the years had become a soft, gently sloping, green verge of grass and moss wide enough for a man to lie on with only his feet stretched out on the bare rock. They lounged there now in a row—Maclean, Leveret, Ginger, Jimmy, and Bill—looking lazily out at the river flowing below them, at the hills on the far side of the river with their farms and orchards, at the highway bridge downriver with its slow-moving freight of Saturday traffic.

The first bottle of ruby red port had gone twice around

quickly and now stood, carefully capped against spillage, between Leveret's knees. The other three bottles in brown paper bags lay in a little hollow among the bushes behind them. The afternoon sunlight, falling through the leaves, lay warm along them, and Maclean, with the warmth also of the port inside him, felt weightless, content, without a care in the world. This beat all to hell sitting in the Legion with the noise and the smoke, so that you could hardly breathe, listening to the same, tired stories, most of them lies, that went round and round until most of the boys there no longer knew the difference between what had really happened in the war and all the bullshit they had made up or seen in the movies.

"Now this is good, boys, ain't it?" Leveret proclaimed. "If this ain't good, boys, then there ain't nothin' good in the world."

Maclean looked across the river at a great, plain, wooden building, like a barn with some extra windows let into it. His first school. How many years ago? The school yard was bordered at the back by a line of sugar maples, and he saw that the whole side of one had already turned a flaming, autumnal red. Funny how some of them always go early like that. Beginning to die and feeling already the coming of winter.

At his age and with his health, whenever the first snow came and the fierce, bone-chilling cold, he always had to wonder whether he would see another spring. ("Will she last the winter?" the daughters whispered to Drusilla, standing outside the door of Mrs. Fraser's room. "No," Drusilla whispered back, "when they get this low, they don't last long." And Mrs. Fraser, her mouth open, a dark hole like the mouths of the three-day dead, lay in her bed, listening and looking up at the ceiling, pretending not to hear.)

He looked across the river, now blue under this blue sky, and imagined it as it would be in four months, a wilderness of ice, the wind howling across it, the way it had the day the old Queen died, and he had stood over there listening to the bells.

"Well, now," Jimmy said, "why don't we send that bottle around another trip?"

Leveret unscrewed the cap and passed the bottle to Maclean, and the bottle went along, each one of them taking his swig, each swig by long practice as near alike as made any difference among pals.

"You just finish that off," Leveret said when the bottle reached Bill, "seein' as you put in a little more than the rest of us."

Bill tipped it up and drained it, then turned the neck down, and they watched as three red drops fell one by one into the moss at his feet. Jimmy took the bottle and went out into the middle of the rock. He made a couple of awkward little sideways jumps and sent the bottle arching end over end out into the river. It went in neck first, bobbed up and over, took enough water to make it float straight up, and began its way slowly downriver towards the bridge and the island.

"We should put a message in one," Ginger said. "We should write our name and address on a piece of paper and put it in and put the cap on. I heard about somebody did that, and somebody found it somewhere way down in the States and wrote back a letter."

"Did he git any money?" Jimmy asked.

"No," Ginger said. "I never heard about no money. But it was in the newspapers and all."

"You should say you're a starvin' orphan," Jimmy said, "and then maybe they'd send ya some money."

Maclean sat with his elbows on his knees watching the bottle as it drifted slowly away from the shore out towards the main channel. He imagined it clearing the rocky shore of the island and sailing on downriver past other islands, past Fredericton, through the Reversing Falls and Saint John Harbour, out into the Bay of Fundy, on and on southwards towards islands of perpetual warmth and sunshine.

Past the lighthouse, past the nunbuoy,
Past the crimson, rising sun,
There are dreams go down the harbour
With the tall ships of Saint John.

"Well, no," Ginger was saying. "I wouldn't want to tell no lies. But I could say that I wouldn't mind comin' to visit them, and maybe if it wasn't too far off, they might send me the money."

"Yes. Well," Leveret said. "I wouldn't be packin' my suitcases just yet for a while."

"It was just an idea," Ginger said. "I ain't never been further than Fredericton once when I went down with the river gang."

Maclean lost sight of the bottle and couldn't find it again among the reflections dancing on the surface of the water, and he sat looking instead at the highway bridge—twelve spans of steel girders looping across the river, high up on tall granite piers beyond the reach of the floodwaters that had carried away an older bridge ten years before he was born. The traffic made two almost solid lines—wagons, cars, trucks—crawling past each other on the narrow roadway conceived before the advent of the motor car and the truck.

Leveret took a second bottle out of its paper bag and unscrewed the cap in his slow, deliberate way, as if it were an operation that required expert deliberation and skill. Ginger took the empty bag and blew it full of air and hit it with the flat of his hand making a sound like a shot, and a flock of waxwings that had been feasting on chokecherries in the bushes behind them exploded upwards and flew off upriver, their tail flashes brilliant in the sunlight.

The bottle went along the line again, the first time quickly, then twice more, more slowly, reflectively. When it was empty, Ginger put it in the sun at the tip of the rock to dry out. Bill had a little notebook, and he tore out a page and wrote Ginger's name on it.

"Ginger Coile, General Delivery, Wakefield, NB, Canada." Ginger rolled the paper up and put it inside the bottle and screwed the cap on tight and threw it out into the river, twice as far as Jimmy had thrown the first one.

With the cap on, it didn't drink any water and floated on its side, tipped down only a little at the bottom, turning its neck slowly around in the current as if looking for the best way to go. Ginger sat down on the edge of the rock and watched it floating away.

"Where do ya think it'll git to, Ginger?" Jimmy asked him.

"I dunno," Ginger said. "But it would be fun if somebody did write me, now wouldn't it."

"And sent ya a ticket to New York City," Jimmy said.

"Or maybe someplace down south," Ginger said, "where nobody don't need to do no work because everythin' they need they can just pick off a tree. That would be great, wouldn't it?"

"Did you hear about the McIntyre boy?" Leveret asked Maclean.

"Yes," Maclean said. "Sam Kelly told me."

"You used to know Timmy McIntyre," Leveret said to Ginger.

"Yes," Ginger said. "We worked on the railroad once for a while."

"He got killed," Leveret said. "In Sicily."

"Oh, Jesus," Ginger said. "That's too bad. What they gonna do with him? They gonna bring him back?"

"No," Leveret explained. "They don't do that. They'll just bury him over there someplace."

"If there's anything to bury," Maclean said.

"Do you remember Sergeant Akers?" Leveret asked.

"Yes," Maclean said. "I haven't thought about him in a long time."

"We used to call him Sergeant Death, remember?"

"Yes," Maclean said. "And a lot of other things too."

Hubert, I am, when I'm 'ome among real human beings, but Sergeant Akers to you bastards. All of a sudden, the glass of memory wiped clean by alcohol, Maclean could see Akers' face as clearly as if it only been an hour ago that he had watched him arrive with his miserable lackeys, boys who had been hauled up for something or other and given to Akers for a week or two as their punishment. A square, lantern jaw, a thin-lipped straight mouth, high cheekbones, a high forehead, and a thin swatch of wispy hair combed straight from one side to the other and held down by some kind of grease. A small man with narrow shoulders, short arms, and white, pudgy, little hands with fingers that looked like disinterred grubs.

He was English—from London, someone said—but he had emigrated to Toronto and joined the Canadian Army there. Maybe because he was no use for anything else, more likely because he went after what no one else wanted, not even as a way to escape getting killed, he was put in charge of burial details for the battalion. He collected whatever bodies or bits of bodies could be collected without too much danger, identified them if he could, and either buried them on the spot or carted them back to the rear.

"Who the hell," Jimmy asked, "was Sergeant Death?"

"Sergeant Death was the guy used to bury our dead men," Leveret told him. "And he loved it, didn't he, Pinky?"

"Yes," Maclean said.

"There was sumpin' very peculiar about him," Leveret said. "Very peculiar. Do you think maybe he was a fruit?"

"Maybe," Maclean said.

"Remember the day the trench got hit with that there mortar bomb," Leveret said, and a whole bunch of the boys got killed?"

"I remember," Maclean said.

"And when Akers got there," Leveret said, squinting out at the river as if trying to get it all in focus, "he said sumpin' queer, and one of the boys was going to knock his head in with a rifle butt. Got himself put on a charge. Remember?"

A great hole smoking like a pit in hell, and naked and half-naked bodies and bits of bodies, blood and guts everywhere, all mixed together with burst sandbags and bits of splintered wood. They got out the boys who had only been wounded, but the dead were all still there when Akers arrived with his crew. And when he came around the corner of the traverse and saw the bodies, he stopped dead in his tracks and stared at them as if all of a sudden there was no one else there but just him and them.

Once somewhere behind the lines in some village with most of its houses blown up, some Frenchman had a girl show. No music or anything like that. Just these women who came out and flounced around on the stage and pulled their dresses up with nothing underneath but their black-haired crotches. And the soldiers, their eyes glued to those white bellies and fat, white legs above black stockings, and those black-haired crotches, had a stunned, stupid look as if all of a sudden they had been deprived of their wits.

That was the look on Akers' face that day as he stood looking at those naked and half-naked dead men.

One of his crew was a boy who couldn't have been more than eighteen, and when he saw the bodies, he went as white as a sheet and started to shake. One of the bodies was lying face down across a pile of dirt with all its clothes blown off, and Akers said to the boy, 'Don't that remind you of your girlfriend?' The boy turned around and puked until it looked as if he was going to die. That was when one of the boys went after Akers with his rifle butt. They got hold of him before he did any damage, but Akers reported him anyway, and he got three days' pack drill.

"'Ash-cans' was what we used to call them mortar bombs," Maclean said to Leveret.

"That's right," Leveret said. "You got a better memory than I have. You even used to be able to talk to them Frenchmen

a little, didn't you? They was sumpin', wasn't they? Them and
the god-damned English. Wasn't they just sumpin' too. And
their god-damned officers with their fuckin' airs. Wonder
somebody didn't shoot 'em."

You men, you men there, what are you doing here? Get
out where you belong. Lieutenant! Lieutenant whatever-
your name is! You there! These men of yours have mud on
their boots! Try to make them look a little more like soldiers.
You Canadians are a disgrace to His Majesty's uniform.

Once somewhere near Festubert, they sent them an
English lieutenant. They'd been marched half the night in
full pack, first this way and then that, listening to shell fire
and machine guns off ahead, all of them hoping to Christ it
would be over before they got there. A mile or more behind
the line, their lieutenant and five of the boys were killed
by shrapnel, and soldiers were scattered all over the place.
Floundering around in the dark, cursing and falling over
each other, they got themselves back together again, more
or less, and settled down in one of the rear support trenches
and went to sleep.

When they woke up, they found they now had this English
lieutenant. He didn't look more than twenty years old, and
he was as smooth-faced as a girl. But he was all dressed up
in a spanking, new officer's uniform out of a London tailor
shop, and he was carrying a cane and a fucking great revolver
that he probably didn't know one end of from the other. It
was as plain as death that he'd never been in the line before
that morning. He had been dug out of some headquarters
somewhere probably, and here was his chance to show what

he was made of and do his bit for King and Country. Except that he was scared out of his mind. You could tell the minute you looked at him that he was going to get himself killed and that he knew it. He was like a man walking in his sleep. Or a man about to be put in front of a firing squad.

That day was one of the worst he could remember. Attacks. Counter attacks. Torrents of shells coming down from every direction. Machine guns firing from every direction. And them sitting there in that trench, getting peppered with shrapnel and having the shit scared out of them by high explosives, no one knowing where they were or what the hell was going on.

Half way through the morning, they were ordered up through a maze of communication trenches to the main support trench. The Germans, it turned out, had just taken the forward trench, and the boys who had been in it and weren't already dead were holding out in shell holes and back along the communication trenches. It was their job to join up with them and re-take the forward trench before the Germans had time to consolidate it.

The English general who had come to inspect them, whoever he was—they all looked and talked the same—stood on a little platform with a swagger stick under his arm and shouted at them in a high-pitched voice, "If you lose a trench, there is to be no hesitation, no waiting for orders. The standing order is that it is to be re-taken immediately at the point of the bayonet. The point of the bayonet, you understand." And he stood up on tiptoes on his little platform and stabbed at the air with his swagger stick.

Captain Bolton gave the order, and over they went, not standing up or any of that craziness, but over and into the first shell hole and then the next one and some of them working along the communication trenches throwing mills bombs. Everybody except the English lieutenant. When the order was given to go over, he gave a shout and climbed over the parapet and went charging ahead waving the cane and the revolver. The Germans were so surprised by this fit of suicidal lunacy that they let him run fifty yards or more before they turned a machine gun on him. The blood flew, and he went ass over teakettle down into a shell hole.

They lost a third of the company, dead and wounded, in the attack. But somewhere down the line, one of the other companies got back into the forward trench, and the Germans in front of their company started trying to get back to their own line before they got cut off. A lot of them were picked off as they tried to make it from shell hole to shell hole, and some of them were hit by their own machine gun fire.

When the boys got back into the forward trench, there weren't any Canadians left alive. Some of the dead men who had been badly wounded had been bayoneted too, and the boys figured that the only way that could have happened was that the Germans had gone around and bayoneted wounded men who couldn't resist. There were three wounded Germans left in the trench, and the boys shot them. One of them, Maclean remembered, had been shot in both legs, and he was half-sitting against one of the angles of a traverse. He had lost his helmet, and you could see that he wasn't more than twenty years old, blond-haired, blue-eyed, as smooth faced and innocent-looking as the English lieutenant back in the shell hole.

"Bitte. Bitte. Bitte," he kept saying.

Some of the boys felt sorry for him and were for letting him off, but there was a big man named Nelson who had lost one of his pals in the attack, and he said, "Bitte, yourself, you little son of a whore, you bayoneted our boys."

And he shot him between the eyes and blew the whole back of his head off.

When Captain Bolton came along and asked what the shooting was about, Nelson said, "They resisted, sir."

Bolton knew well enough what had happened, but he had seen the bayoneted men too, and he said, "All right, but no more."

Sometimes, if no one was attacking anyone else, the Germans and Canadians let each other get in their wounded, but everyone was too mad this time to do that, so a lot of the wounded in the open had to lie there until dark. Then the boys managed to get in all the ones who were still alive without losing anybody doing it. Their dead men, including the English lieutenant, they shoveled some dirt over and marked with a piece of board in case they wanted to try to get them later. The dead Germans they left. They were going to stink, but there was no sense getting killed over a stink.

Everyone expected another artillery barrage the next morning and another attack. But the next morning nothing happened except a lot of random rifle and machine-gun fire. The day after that they were pulled back for their three days out. In fact, they were out for over a week while they were brought back up to strength. When they got back, the trenches had been fixed up, but the bodies, half-buried Canadians and what the rats had left of the unburied Germans, were still out there between the support trench and the forward trench.

Then one afternoon, a few days after they got back into the line, two English majors and a lieutenant arrived in the support trench along with Captain Bolton and their new lieutenant, named Archie Macleod, one of the best while they had him.

One of the majors was the father of the English lieutenant who had got himself killed in the counter-attack, and he had come to get his son's body. He was a fat little man who didn't look any more like a soldier than Miss Audrey Sweet, and he must have had some kind of staff job somewhere to have enough pull to get permission to do what he was doing. It wasn't a healthy time to be chasing around out there looking for bodies, but Bolton was only a captain and Macleod was only a lieutenant, and they were two majors and English besides.

You wouldn't have lasted ten seconds out there in daylight, so they sat around in Bolton's dugout until it got dark, and it was arranged that Macleod and a couple of the boys who had buried the English lieutenant would go out for him. The English lieutenant who had come along with the father and who looked as if he had never seen a trench before either, wanted to go too, to demonstrate his bravery no doubt, but Bolton refused that at least, saying he didn't know the ground and would be a danger to his men.

So Macleod and the two boys sneaked out of the communication trench through one of the holes that had been blown in it. They took a little lantern covered over with a ground sheet that they could use to make sure they had the right body without showing any light the Germans might see. But the Germans saw something anyway, and ten minutes later there was a great rattle of machine gun fire.

"Them fuckin' pongos are gonna get us all killed," somebody muttered.

But there wasn't any mortaring, just the machine gun fire, and after a while that let up, and just when it was beginning to look as if Macleod and the others had been caught by the machine guns, the word went along the trench that they were back.

He had been there himself in the little crowd that had gathered just where the communication trench came into the support trench. The two boys came in dragging the body on the ground sheet followed by Macleod. The body had been out there for a week and half by then, and the face was getting rotten, but you could tell who it was all right if you knew him. The Englishmen had never seen any of this before, nor even imagined it—the dirt, the slime, the rubbish, the stink, let alone what a week-and-a-half-old body looked like that had been machine-gunned and left to rot in the mud.

The three of them stood there looking down at it. The lieutenant, the stupid bastard, saluted it. The father just looked. Then he dropped down on his knees on the duckboards and started to cry. "My son, my son, my son." As a staff officer, he had probably filled the boy full of bullshit about King and Country and the charge of the god-damned Light Brigade. Still you couldn't help feeling sorry for him. It went on and on. He just collapsed. After a while, the other major got him to his feet, and they got the body onto a stretcher, and a couple of the boys went off down the trench with it with the Englishmen shuffling along behind like drunk men. Crazy.

He'd never had the faintest idea what that battle was about, and neither had anybody else he'd ever talked to. When histories of the war began to come out, he found one in the Legion and looked through it, but all he could find out about what was going on around Festubert at the time was a reference to some "brisk" skirmishes. Whatever all the killing had been about that day, it evidently hadn't qualified as history. Maybe somebody had delivered orders to the wrong people, and it only got noticed after a couple of days. Maybe some general on one side or the other had decided that things had been too quiet and that soldiers would lose their edge if more of them weren't getting killed.

He found a bottle, their third bottle, once again in his hand. It had been going back and forth, and he had been drinking without noticing. Now there was left in it only one small swig. He tipped it, and rolled the warm, sweet wine around in his mouth before swallowing it.

All that stuff was a long time ago, and long gone, and he had survived when there had been many times he never thought he would, when he saw himself lying dead out there, no different from the mud he was lying in his mud-coloured uniform.

He lay back against the bank and put his hands under his head and closed his eyes. The waxwings that Buster had scared off blowing up the paper bag had come back to the chokecherry bushes and were fluttering and chirruping behind him. From far away, he could hear the sound of the traffic on the bridge, a mere whisper, like the rustle of leaves, in the intervals of the lazy talk beside him, Bill explaining to Jimmy how to use some old shingles he had found thrown away somewhere to roof his woodshed, Leveret huffing and snuffling like an old dog, now and then treating Ginger to some profundity that had risen to his mind. ("Now this here, Ginger, is Saturday, and tomorrow's going to be Sunday.") Ginger silent, moving his boots around now and then on the rock, thinking maybe about his wine bottle on its way to the sunlit islands where he would go and never have to load another barrel of potatoes.

With the sunlight falling through the leaves on his face, Maclean drifted into a dreamless sleep.

6

It was the birds that woke him, a storm of wings over his head, like the sound of a sudden rain among leaves, followed at once by the rattle and crunch of boots on the clinkers at the top of the path near the tracks.

Leveret whipped the last bottle of port up from the grass behind him and put it inside his coat and lay back against the bank, tucking the bottle between his right arm and his body and putting his good hand in the pocket of his coat to hold the bottle in place in case he had to get up.

They saw the legs first, two pairs of them sliding down the steep path, then from between the bushes and out onto the rock, the two men entire: Willie Campbell and, close behind, Junior Tedley, who in his brainless way had shouted after Maclean on Main Street that morning when he was trying to make it back to his dinner.

Willie Campbell was short, thick-set, big-muscled. Black hair, thick black eyebrows, a three- or four-day growth of black beard, hairy black arms, black everything, including a black heart. He had a little farm across the river, and a skinny, sickly, little wife who was pregnant all the time, and a brood of dirty kids. After he had been drinking for a while, he had a way of turning ugly, and once he started drinking, he never stopped until he ran out or drank himself insensible. It was when he was still on his feet and had nothing left to drink that he was at his ugliest.

Junior Tedley was a clown—tall, thin, except for a little beer-belly and a fat ass, with bug eyes and a great, foolish, turned-down moustache that he kept stroking one side of, the way he had seen some gun-fighter do in a cowboy movie.

They came down so fast that nobody had time to get up, and they were all still half-sitting, half-lying against the bank when Willie emerged from the path to confront them, his eyes going everywhere, looking for a bottle, and also probably sizing up what he might be in for if he made trouble.

"Well," he said in a voice which always had a snarl at the edge of it. "Looks like quite a little party goin' on here."

"No, no," Jimmy said. "Nothin' like that. We just been settin' here soakin' up a little sun and talkin' about the world."

"Are you makin' fun of me?" Willie said, turning on him.

"No," Jimmy said, scrambling to his feet. "Just tellin' ya the kind of time we been havin'."

"Bullshit," Willie said.

He turned on Leveret.

"I hear ya just about bought out the liquor store down there this afternoon," he said.

"I don't know about that," Leveret said. "We got three bottles of port for the five of us here, and we drunk 'em all up."

"I don't see no empty bottles," Willie said.

"One there in the bushes," Leveret said. "We threw the other two in the river."

"We put a note in one with my name on it," Ginger said.

"And if somebody finds it, they're maybe gonna write me a letter."

Willie paid no attention to him and turned on Maclean.

"I hear you insulted my cousin here this mornin'," he said. "Right there on Main Street where everybody could hear."

He gestured at Junior, who stood beside him stroking his moustache and looking foolish, then made a move towards Maclean.

Maclean got to his feet to stay clear of any boots that might come flying his way, and Leveret and Bill got up too. Only Ginger went on sitting, still thinking about the bottle with the note in it.

"I didn't know Junior was your cousin," Jimmy said.

"Well, you know it now," Willie said without looking at him.

"So what have ya got to say?" he asked Maclean.

"Willie," Maclean said, "don't talk such horseshit. Junior isn't any more your cousin than I am."

"Are you callin' me a liar?" Willie shouted at him. "Or my cousin here?"

"I said 'hello' and you told me to fuck off," Junior said.

"I was in hurry," Maclean said. "I didn't even look to see who it was."

"You lyin' bastard," Willie said.

He put his fists up and shuffled towards Maclean like a boxer moving in for the kill.

Time was when Maclean could have beaten the shit out of Willie Campbell, but that time was long gone. He put one arm up to protect himself and backed away, but there wasn't much space to back to. Watching Willie, not where he was going, he slipped on the damp moss at the edge of the rock, and before he could catch himself fell half sideways down through the bushes. The branches scraped his face as he went down, and he hit the side of his head against something, an old stump or a rock.

In two seconds he was back on his legs and fishing around in his pocket for his jack knife.

"Now, look here," Leveret said, "there ain't no call for this. We ain't done you no harm."

Willie turned on him.

"What kind of god-damned man are you," he said, "wouldn't give a man a drink on a Saturday afternoon? What kind of god-damned man is that?"

He was working himself into a black rage, and Maclean could see that he wanted to fight now more than drink. While he wasn't watching, Maclean opened the main blade of his jack knife, three inches long and well sharpened, and put it back in his pocket out of sight. He had no intention of cutting Willie if he didn't have to, but he could use it to keep him off.

Leveret backed away from Willie, and the neck of the port bottle tilted over and stuck out from the front of his coat.

"You lyin' old fucker," Willie growled. "So you drunk it all up, did ya?"

He glared straight into Leveret's eyes. Then drew back and hit him across the side of the face with the back of his hand.

He didn't swing very hard, but he drove Leveret's upper lip back against his teeth and a heavy drop of blood oozed out and down onto his chin. His hat went flying, and Jimmy caught up with it just before it went over the edge of the rock into the river.

Ginger watched all this with puzzlement, not sure that it wasn't all just some kind of game, that Willie wasn't just making believe he was angry, that all the name-calling wasn't just rough affection, like saying, "you old son of a bitch, how are ya?" For a second or two, it even looked as if he thought that Leveret's lip getting split was just a rough and tumble accident, the kind of thing that happened sometimes among pals with no harm meant. It was only when he saw Leveret stagger off to one side with his hand up to his face and saw Jimmy chasing after Leveret's precious hat and heard Bill Kayton shout, "You dirty bastard, hitting an old man," that he realized that Willie had really attacked his idol.

He bellowed and heaved himself to his feet and went after Willie, his big fists, the size of bowling balls, waving around in the air in front of him. In open ground, Willie could have stayed away from him, but there wasn't much room to move around on top of the rock and not go over the side, and Ginger was on top of him before he could even get his fists up.

They wrestled around, Willie trying to keep his feet under him and not go over the side, cursing all the time, spit foaming at the corners of his mouth, Ginger bellowing and grabbing at anything he could get his hands on, intent only on killing Willie even if they did both go over the side.

Willie got a little space between them and drove his knee up into Ginger's balls. Ginger howled and doubled over and let go of Willie, and Willie got a punch in somewhere on Ginger's face. Ginger grabbed his arm with both hands and tried to break it the way you might snap a stick, and they both went down, half into the bushes and half out, Willie cursing, Ginger growling like an enraged bear.

While all this was going on, Junior was prancing around like a ten-year-old. Now he turned on Jimmy and put his fists up. Jimmy skipped out of his way and picked up a rock the size of a baseball.

"You come near me," Jimmy said, " and by the whistlin', blue-eyed Jesus, I'll knock your fuckin' brains out."

Willie had got astride Ginger and was trying to pry Ginger's arms clear of his face to get in another punch. Leveret, hatless, still oozing blood, passed the bottle to Bill and got a big stick of wood from a fallen tree, four feet long and as thick as a man's arm but starting to rot into a brown pulpiness. He lurched over and broke the stick across Willie's shoulders. It was too rotten to hurt him much, but it put him off his guard long enough for Ginger to heave him off and come down on top of him. Ginger put both fists together and brought them down on Willie's forehead and smashed his head back against the rock.

"You better git Ginger off," Leveret said, "or he's gonna kill him."

"That's enough, Ginger," Bill said, taking Ginger by the shoulder.

Ginger didn't want to stop. He hit Willie in the face again with a closed fist, like a man pounding on a table, before Bill got his arm and eased him off.

"Get the hell out of here," Bill said to Willie, "or he's going to kill you and end up in jail."

Willie got himself up. He was bleeding out of his mouth now too, bleeding and spitting, with snot running down from his nose into the blood.

"I'll git you fuckers," he snarled. "Just you wait. You gang up on me, but I'll git you fuckers one by one."

He lunged forward with one foot towards Maclean, and Maclean drew the open jack knife out of his pocket and waved it in front of him.

"You draw a knife on me, you bastard," Willie shouted.

"He don't mean nothin'," Leveret said. "He's just tryin' to protect himself. Now why don't you go on back to town before there's any more trouble."

"I still ain't had no drink," Willie said.

"You're not going to get a drink either," Bill said. "That's all we got left, and there's five of us."

"Suppose I just take it," Willie said.

"You try to take it," Bill said, "and we'll beat the shit out of you."

Maclean knew that if Willie got hold of the bottle, they might not get it back, but if that was the price of getting rid of the son of a whore, it might be worth it. Drawing the knife, he was telling himself, had been stupid.

"Well," Leveret said, "if it's O.K. with the other boys, it's O.K. with me. But just one swig and then you git out of here and leave us alone."

He looked at Bill.

Bill shrugged.

He passed the bottle to Leveret, and Leveret unscrewed the cap and passed it to Willie. He wiped the blood and snot from his mouth and tipped the bottle back and drank, swallow after swallow without breathing.

"Now, that's enough," Leveret said, and Bill went over and took the bottle away from him, cautiously, as if he were taking a bone away from a cross dog. It would be like Willie to throw the bottle and what was left in it into the river, but he let Bill take it.

"Junior's gotta have one too," Willie said.

"One," Bill said and passed the bottle to Junior.

He tipped the bottle up, and after one swallow, Bill took the bottle away from him. Between the two of them, they had half emptied it.

"O.K.," Bill said. "Now get out of here."

"Now don't go orderin' me around," Willie said, "or I may take it into my head to spend the rest of the afternoon here."

"Just you go on, now," Leveret said, "before someone gets hurt again."

Willie stood long enough to satisfy his honour, then turned.

"Come on, Junior," he said. "I've had enough of these cheap cocksuckers."

They started up the path. Ginger would have gone after them, but Leveret stopped him.

Bill looked at the bottle. There was blood and snot on the neck, and Christ knows what else. He passed the bottle to Leveret, and Leveret pulled some leaves off one of the chokecherry bushes and wiped it as clean as he could, then gave it a final polish with his handkerchief.

"There," he said. "Clean as it came from the store."

He offered it to Bill, but Bill shook his head.

"Someone should kill that son of a whore," Bill said.

"I expect some day someone will," Maclean said.

They sat down, and the bottle went back and forth between the other three until they finished it. Ginger took it out to the tip of the rock and threw it into the river. No one was paying much attention. Ginger watched it bobbing around only a dozen yards from shore. He came back and sat down.

"I expect that bottle with the note in it will just fetch up somewheres," he said.

They had settled themselves down in a different pattern, Leveret, Ginger, and Jimmy together, Leveret with his hat back on, his cut lip still oozing a little blood, Maclean and Bill a little way off.

"You all right?" Bill asked Maclean. "You look like you got a bump on your head."

"It ain't nothing," Maclean said. "Take more than that to kill me."

"I expect," Bill said.

But the truth was that he wasn't feeling good at all. His head hurt, his back hurt, his stomach had turned queasy, and there loomed above him the thought that although Willie was gone, there would be more to it some other day. The knife had been stupid.

"The son of a whore," Bill said.

Maclean looked at him out of the corner of his eye. He was a good-looking man. Thick, brown hair, always combed. Good features. Dress him up in a suit, and he could have been a businessman or a lawyer, a movie actor even. But if you looked close, you could see the skin going slack under the eyes, and the lids a little puffed-up and a little too pink. The booze starting to take its toll. Maclean wondered how old he was. Thirty maybe, maybe a little less. About the age he had been when he lost his last real job and gave up or gave in or whatever.

He felt he ought to say something to Bill. Though he probably didn't know it, Bill was on the edge. Once over, it was tough to climb back. When the war was over, and there were lots of men and not much work the way it was after the Great War, they would be able to get good carpenters who didn't drink, so why should they hire ones like Bill who did? So you would drink because you didn't have a job, and people wouldn't give you a job because you drank, and so it would go around.

So what should he say to Bill? Get yourself together. Stop drinking. Work steady. Get a good wife. Have children. Stay at home nights and listen to the radio. Or take your wife to a movie. Or work in your garden or your carpentry shop in the back shed. Go to church. Join a lodge. Be an upstanding member of the community. Live so that when you die, everybody will say nice things about you and give you a big funeral.

"You do have to wonder sometimes," Henry said, "what life is supposed to be all about, now don't you.?"

"It ain't about anything," Maclean said. "It ain't about a god-damned thing."

"No," Henry said. "There has to be a purpose to it. It just stands to reason."

"Like God," Maclean said.

"That's right," Henry said. "Like God."

Maclean dug at the moss-covered earth in front of him with the heel of his boot and uncovered a colony of tiny black insects, which went chasing around in the ruins of their world looking for somewhere to get back underground out of danger.

He looked out across the river at the climbing flame of red maple leaves behind the old school and remembered the first day he had gone there, setting out on a bright, summery

September morning with Alice, who was already in Grade Four, a smart girl in school, pretty as pretty could be, with great, brown eyes and long, brown hair. (Once when he was little he said that he was going to marry her when he grew up, and his mother had laughed.) He had a bookbag and a slate that his mother had bought him early that summer so she could teach him his letters before he started school. Life was beginning for him, and he felt important and afraid, marching along the road beside Alice.

Other children strung out along the road ahead of them and behind, and a big old wagon passing them with a load of hay, and a man leading a little herd of cows across the road to a pasture on the riverbank, and the river flowing away beside them, and the town on the far side climbing its hill with the steeples and the town clock at the top, and this rock there too jutting out black from the bank of green, waiting for them to come and be sitting here today and waiting too for the time when they would all be swept away and forgotten.

7

Maclean trudged, head down, eyes front, uphill past big old houses with oak front doors and bay windows, wide lawns and carefully weeded flower beds. It was the kind of street he didn't like walking on and only did when there was no other, even half-easy way to get where he was going, the kind of street that gave him the feeling of being watched by indignant ladies peeking out at him from behind curtains or through the wickering of trellises or gazebos, a shabby trespasser in their manicured world, a breath of undeodorized humanity from the alleys, a reminder even, in his skeletal lineaments and the evident fragility and brevity of his expectations, of the dust and mud and rot that all this tidiness was designed to allow them to forget.

At the crest of the hill, the big houses and the sidewalk abruptly ended, and the pavement gave way to a rough gravel road with ditches on either side, half-filled with brown, peaty water where beetles skimmed and tiny frogs kerflopped and vanished into the roots of the bordering weeds as he passed. Beyond a little buffer zone of uncut black firs, houses began again, but smaller and poorer now, some of them hardly more than shacks, on little lots cut out of the woods with unpulled stumps sometimes at the back and a general rawness of ground which gave the whole place the feel of being somewhere much further from the centre of town than it was.

Alice's house was on the right, half a dozen houses on and set back a little from the road so that it was hidden by the house before it. Maclean approached cautiously, close over to the right beside the ditch, watching for the first glimpse, if there was to be one, of Mitch's half-ton truck. The wonderful lightness of the early part of the afternoon had been driven away, leaving behind it something half way between drunkenness and hung-over sobriety. As he came up to the house beside Alice's, he saw that Mitch's parking spot was empty, and he swung out into the middle of the road and began to walk as best he could like a man drawn along by nothing more than a casual, summer-afternoon fancy for a little stroll.

Alice's house sat sideways to the road and consisted mostly of afterthoughts. When Mitch bought it, fifteen years before, it was just a bungalow, but as their brood of kids grew Mitch pushed out rooms this way and that and finally added to the original structure a second-storey with an almost flat roof which had to be shoveled all winter to keep it from collapsing.

Maclean crossed into the yard on a culvert of old railroad ties and made his way around to the back of the house. He mounted the steps to the kitchen door and peeked in through the screen. Alice had become a little deaf and hadn't heard him arrive. She was standing with her back to the door cooking doughnuts in a great pot of boiling fat on a black woodstove. There were pans and bowls everywhere, a cookie sheet with ginger snaps, a pan of johnnie cake, an uncooked pie.

Alice had undergone a succession of transfigurations since Maclean had gone off to the war. When he first came back, she was still a good-looking woman, not much different from the good-looking woman he had last seen when he left. Then after she had had six children, she became gaunt and worn and looked more like fifty years old than thirty-five. Then some years later, some female thing happened inside her, and she had ballooned in a couple of years to her present size and come to look the fifty she now was, only a different kind of fifty.

She was wearing an old, flowered, short-sleeve print dress, hoisted up higher in the back than in the front by her hips and streaked with sweat under the armpits and down the middle of the back. Her arms and legs were fat and white, her legs were pebbled with varicose veins, her hair was graying and thinning, hanging as straight and slack as a bunch of strings.

Maclean tapped on the screen door, first gently, then a little harder.

Alice looked back over her shoulder, and he caught the look of surprise, then, unmistakably, of aggravation as she recognized him. He thought of saying 'hello' and then leaving, but he found himself already opening the door, taking off his cap, and stepping inside into the heat and the rich smell of frying doughnuts.

"I was just going by out here on the road," he said, "and I thought I'd look in for a minute. I didn't get you at a very good time."

"I can't stop these now," she shouted, all flustered. "Once I got them started, I can't stop."

"No, no," he said. "I can see that. Don't you trouble."

He fidgeted uncertainly at the door, wondering if he should go away after all, while Alice went on dropping in doughnuts, turning them, fishing them out, not looking at him, her movements abrupt and awkward.

"You gonna sit down?" she asked finally.

"Well," he said, "just for a few minutes maybe, then I've got to be going."

He edged past her, his cap in his hand, and sat in a chair by the window, where she could see him to talk to while she worked.

She leaned forward and stared at him.

"What have you done to your face?" she asked. "You ain't been in a fight?"

"I don't know," he said. "Something wrong?"

He got up and looked at himself in the mirror over the sink. There was a bruise, black and blue, on the side of his forehead where he had hit it when he fell at the Black Rock, and a scratch down one cheek and some dirt on his chin.

"I was working down at Jim Gartley's stable," he said, "and I bumped my head against one of the beams along the side of a stall."

He ran a little water into a pan in the sink, washed and dried his face, and went back to his place by the window.

There was a teapot on the back of the stove, but Alice didn't offer to pour any, and she didn't offer him a doughnut either. He reflected that she probably didn't want to encourage him to stay in case Mitch came back from the store for some reason. Or one of the girls dropped in.

"Tomorrow's mother's birthday," he said.

"Yes," Alice said. "August 22."

She lifted out another batch of doughnuts and shuffled

her feet around on the floor.

"That's why I looked for the job at Jim Gartley's," he said. "So I could buy her a little something."

She looked hard at him. And so you could buy yourself some liquor, the look said.

"How long did you work for Jim?" she asked.

"Just an hour or so. He doesn't have a lot to do there, and I just rubbed down one or two of the horses for him. But I got enough for a present."

"Well, that's good," she said, and he could see she was beginning to relent.

She moved the pot of fat off the stove and started stirring something up in a big, brown mixing bowl that had been in the kitchen across the river for as long as Maclean could remember.

"Little Ruthie ain't been too well the last week or two," she said, changing the subject. "Some kind of summer cold or somethin'. She ain't very strong that child."

"I guess not," Maclean said. "That's too bad."

He remembered seeing Little Ruthie on the street once with her mother—a frail little girl with toothpick arms and legs.

"I always been scared of sickness," Alice said. "Especially with kids. Ever since that awful flu, I always been scared. People as healthy could be on Monday and dead on Friday. Father nearly died of it. It was terrible. And the Skadgets. Just about that whole family. And Elsie, that big healthy girl you wouldn't have thought anything could kill. Remember?"

"Yes," Maclean said. "I remember."

It had been a long time since he had thought of Elsie.

Six o'clock in the morning. The middle of June. At the top of the hill, high above the river, a farmer had an acre of strawberries, and himself and Elsie Skadget and half a dozen others went up to pick for him to make a little money, a cent or two a box. He took them up in the back of his wagon. Halfway up, a mist hung on the hill, and they drove up into it like birds disappearing into the clouds. It was so thick they could hardly see the ditches beside them as they bumped slowly along, the horses labouring on the steep road. Then gradually the mist became bright with diffused sunlight, and suddenly they came out above it on the top of the hill, the sky overhead absolutely cloudless and so bright you could hardly look at it, and below them the great, snow-white carpet of mist stretching off to the hills far away west of the town towards the American border.

He sat beside Elsie in the wagon, and he could feel her hip soft against him, and he didn't know whether she wanted it to be that way or whether it was something she didn't even notice. It must have been 1909. The summer before he went to high school. Without having any idea what he meant by it, he had decided that he was in love with Elsie Skadget, and all that morning as they picked berries and the field grew hot under the sun, he tried to get himself a row next to hers. When they were close together, they talked, and he could remember Elsie's loud laugh and the way the other pickers sometimes looked at them.

Alice had put the mixing bowl on the table and had begun spooning out the dough in little blobs on a cookie sheet.

"Little Ruthie just loves peanut butter cookies," she said.

"Yes," Maclean said. "That's good."

They lived, the Skadgets, on a weedy, two-acre farm on a side hill above the gulch that ran off into the forest from the end of the bridge. The mother was a big, strapping, slovenly woman who always smelled like sour milk, the father, a sad, little man who seemed to spend all day just sitting by the kitchen door watching the chickens. There were eight, maybe even ten kids, it was hard to keep track, and they lived in an unpainted, ramshackle house with only three or four rooms for all of them and not much to keep the wind from blowing through. On cold nights in the winter, people said, they used to bring two or three of their pigs inside to help keep them all from freezing to death.

"Mitch says that peanut butter is one of the best foods in the world."

"That so?" Maclean said.

"Mitch says that if you was shipwrecked on a desert island, the very best thing you could have would be lots of peanut butter."

Elsie Skadget was a year older than he was, and by the time he was thirteen, he began to have thoughts about her that his father would have horsewhipped him for. She wasn't pretty at all, not the kind of girl the poems seemed to be about, nor the kind that decorated the lids of chocolate tins, slim and bosomless, with rosebud lips and corn-silk hair, and skin as white as snow except for the blush of rose on the cheeks, and little oval faces, and delicate little hands. Elsie's mouth was wide and full, her hair black, a great, thick, crinkily mass of it, her skin blemished by chickenpox and by the middle of summer tanned as dark as an Indian's. Even at fourteen, she had heavy breasts and heavy woman's hips that rolled around inside her cotton dress as she walked and made butterflies under Maclean's heart whenever he found himself walking behind her on the road. The boys made coarse jokes about how repulsive she was, and he was too ashamed of what he felt and too young and dumb and blinded by his shame to see that they all lusted after her the same as he did.

All through the hot, heavy days of that summer, the thought of her was never far away, and in the evenings after his two or three hours of chores were finished, and on Sundays when to work was a sin, he usually saw her, along with the gang of kids they were both part of, swimming in the river by a little woodworking shop that had a ramp down into the water or drifting aimlessly up and down the road. Sometimes on Saturday nights, they journeyed the quarter mile across the bridge into town to walk the crowded streets, looking in store windows at all the things they couldn't buy.

"When they don't need me no more at home," Elsie said, "I'm gonna come over here and git a job in one of them stores and buy me a dress just like that one there."

"I tell Ruthie, 'you want to make that girl eat more,'" Alice said. "She needs a little more flesh on them bones. It don't do no harm to be a little fat, Mitch always says, because then you got somethin' to live off if you get sick."

Every year at the end of August, they held the annual exhibition at the park on the big island in the middle of the river, which suddenly became a magical place with a dome of light above it at night and the music from the carnival rides and shows drifting up to them across the water. They went one night, a little crowd of them. They walked around the exhibition sheds at first because they didn't have to pay to do that, looking at the same animals and vegetables they saw every day at home, waiting for it to get dark when the magic of the lights would be at its best before they went in to the carnival. They didn't have enough money to go to the shows, but they stood in the crowd at the front watching the outdoor acts intended to draw them in, fire-eaters and fat ladies and hootchie-kootchie dancers and jugglers. Near the time they had to go home, they spent their money on the rides, some on the Ferris wheel, some on the merry-go-round. As well as the pairs of gaudy horses, the merry-go-round had a gaudy, little wagon that Elsie rode around in by herself, waving at the crowd along the fence like a queen in a procession.

They went back across the bridge in a ragged single file because there was no walk for pedestrians, only the roadway so narrow you had to stand flattened against the railings when something wide was edging its way past something else that was wide. Without really admitting to himself what he was doing, he let himself fall behind, and Elsie fell behind too and walked ahead of him, talking away about the carnival and what she would have done if she'd had more money. He hardly listened, his heart pounding.

When they got to the end of the bridge, the others had all gone their ways into the darkness. He walked with Elsie along the little road that led up the gulch toward the Skadget place. They stopped in the darker darkness under a big maple, and he kissed her, a quick peck on the lips, and mumbled good night and fled away home.

"But them other kids of Ruthie's, they ain't fat nor nothin', but they're just as healthy as can be," Alice said. "It's funny, ain't it. Just no reason."

"No," Maclean said. "I guess most of the time there isn't."

They were sitting on the ramp by the woodworking shop, Elsie in a bathing suit she had made out of an old dress, which when wet, clung to the shape of her nakedness beneath.

"Why don't you come up to our place after supper," Elsie whispered to him, "and we'll go for a walk."

The summer sun still high and hot. They walked up along the edge of a field full of yellow stubble where the last hay had been cut. Two of her younger brothers trailed along behind them further down the hill. One of them ran out into the field waving his arms, and a flock of blackbirds—grackles, starlings, red wings—rose and swirled in a great corkscrew of motion above the hillside and came down again further away. The boy ran after them, and the other boy followed.

They climbed a cedar rail fence, he first, Elsie after, bending over, her breasts hanging loose inside her dress, laughing her hoarse laugh, knowing very well what he was looking at.

"Now her sister Mildred's kids is all just little butterballs," Alice said. "It must have somethin' to do with heredity."

A corner of the next field. Wild grass, buttercups, daisies, devil's paint brushes. The black birds swirling again overhead. The voices of the boys fading away, further off down the hill. Lying close together, finding her naked under her dress, watching her violent fit, unknowing and terrified at first that something awful, something fatal, was happening to her. Later on the way home, overwhelmed with guilt and the fear that his father would find out and horsewhip him or drive him from the house. Sin will always be found out. The righteous can always see it in the faces of the unrighteous as plain as if they were branded.

"Mildred's husband Frank, now he ain't big, but his mother was a big woman if ever there was. Mitch says people take after their grandparents more than their parents"

"Maybe so," Maclean said.

A few days later, they met again at their spot on the hillside, and two or three more times after that. Then in the fall, he went across the river to the high school, feeling clumsy and awkward, the only one in his class there who wasn't a town kid. He was only there a year and a half, but it was enough to make him feel ashamed of what his classmates might say if they knew he had a girlfriend like Elsie Skadget.

Then the war came and later the influenza.

It arrived in George County a few months after he came home from England, first one or two people coming down with it, nobody yet hardly knowing what it was, then more and more, and the atmosphere of terror gathering like that of the Black Death as people started dying when the winter came. People not going out any more than they had to, wearing a whole witch's cupboard of crazy charms.

The Skadgets got it in the middle of the winter, and lying around in that ramshackle house with the wind

blowing through it, every one of them died except the
mother and one boy. Elsie was one of the first. Too many
people were dying for graves to be dug in the frozen ground,
so the undertakers collected the bodies in a barn on the edge
of town after the funeral ceremonies, and in the spring there
were dozens of buryings. The Skadgets were all lowered into
the same grave in plain, wooden coffins on a rainy day with
the water running down the piles of raw earth onto the coffins in the bottom, where a field mouse had fallen in the
night before and drowned.

His father had watched all the dying with fierce satisfac-
tion. It was God's judgement on the wicked and the lazy.
Then he got the influenza himself, the only one in the house
to get it, and nearly died. But the judgement of God, who
is a just God, visits his wrath not only on individuals but on
their houses. Many were the children whose sins God has
punished through the father.

That awful house of self-righteousness and rage as the
winter of 1918 dragged toward spring. Sleet, then snow
again, then rain that froze on everything. The roads so covered with ice that you could hardly stand up on them, then
so deep in mud that a horse would sink to its fetlocks with
every step and give up and just stand. Sometimes with all
that mud and death, it seemed to him as if he was back in
Flanders. Then the ice breaking up at last at the end of April
and the first flowers of spring coming up in the woods. And
all the while, more and more of the boys dragging home
with their wounds, outer and inner, from the trenches.

At the table Alice was rolling little doughnut balls around
on a plate of sugar.

Maclean eyed the cooked doughnuts.

Alice caught the look.

"Them doughnuts is cool now if you want one," she said curtly as if giving an order.

"Thanks," he said. "I wouldn't mind."

He picked out one that had exploded a little in the hot fat and had a thicker, rougher crust on one side.

If he had never gone to high school, he might have married Elsie Skadget and had kids and never gone to the war. And if she had married him, or even if they were just going together when the influenza came, fate might have taken a different road so that she didn't die.

Once he and Henry had one of their long talks on the porch at Drusilla's, and they decided that if even one little thing happened differently, then all sorts of other things would happen differently too. For example, on his way into town, a young man might stop along the road to admire a butterfly and six hours later get killed by a car whereas if he hadn't stopped to look at the butterfly he wouldn't have been stepping onto the street just at the moment when the car was arriving and might have gone on living for another fifty years. He might have gone on to be married. Children might have been born. Other lives lived. All because of a butterfly.

It makes you think, as Henry said.

"Do you remember," Maclean said, "the time the bunch of us walked out to Lake Kintyre to have a picnic? Us two and the Nickerson girls, and Elsie Skadget and one of her brothers."

Alice eyed him over her shoulder, and didn't answer at first, searching maybe for the memory, or maybe not wanting it.

"Yes," she said, finally. "And Sadie and Billy Sprague."

"And Harry Noles," Maclean said and wondered if maybe he shouldn't have mentioned Harry.

"Yes," she said. "And Harry too."

Late July. The road along the little wooded valley dusty and shimmering. The brook that ran beside it so shallow it seemed hardly to be moving at all, as if it were nothing but a network of standing pools among the rocks. The chokecherry bushes along the road heavy with fruit and swarming with robins and blackbirds. The smell of the evergreens on the sides of the valley drifting down through the heat. And the crowd of them tramping along, the boys in caps, the girls in wide-brimmed straw hats with ribbons—except for Elsie Skadget, who had an old straw hat of her father's all raveling away along the brim.

Alice was still taller than he was, slim and straight. She walked with a long, swinging stride beside Harry Noles, and he remembered her laughing. Once she ran away, and Harry chased her up the road until she ran out of breath, and they both stood at the top of a little rise waiting for the rest to catch up.

Where the road skirted the shore of Lake Kintyre before vanishing away into the deep forest, there was a stretch of green and a narrow beach of rounded stones. They sat there in a line on the edge of the green and ate their sandwiches of jam and cheese on homemade bread and looked across the lake at the forest rising up over the hill on the other side. Alice had taken an interest in poetry and once read aloud at the school closing, and she had brought along a book, hoping maybe that Harry Noles would see her as a sensitive and intelligent soul.

"I wandered lonely as a cloud," she read, "that floats on high o'er vales and hills."

Funny that so small a thing could be so great an adventure that he had remembered it all his life when there were now whole years that he couldn't remember one thing about.

What year was it? 1906 maybe. It must have been just about then that Alice finished Grade 8 and father made her leave school. Perhaps that was what reading the poetry that day was about.

"I wandered lonely as a cloud," Maclean said.

"What?" Alice asked, looking up from the stove.

"Nothing," he said.

"Ain't you gonna eat that doughnut?"

"Yes. Yes, I am."

As she went on stirring furiously at something in a double boiler, he slowly ate his doughnut and looked around at the great clutter of cooking gear and fended off as best he could the sense of exile that threatened to assail him.

He became aware that more of the port he had drunk at the Black Rock had begun to work its way through. He wondered if he would be able to make it back to the boarding house without being caught short and decided not.

"I wonder," he asked, "if I could use your bathroom."

8

Maclean peeked over the top of the bathroom curtain at the back yard. A chicken coop, a little vegetable garden, at the back, a dense stand of fir trees unmoving in the afternoon heat, reminding him again of that long-ago morning when Alice at one of life's awful crossroads had read Wordsworth to Harry Noles. Inside, on a set of shelves beside the wash-basin, an arrangement of domestic clutter. Surprise soap. Toothbrushes. Hair brushes. Hair curlers. A pile of neatly folded towels. A shaving mug. A shaving brush. A safety razor. The furnishings of a settled life where a man might lie of an evening in a tub of hot water and read and float away from the troubles outside.

He looked at his face in the mirror. The bruise on his fore-head was getting bigger and turning an even uglier shade of black and blue.

When he first moved to town, he boarded at a nice house on a nice residential street. It belonged to a couple, Bob and Clara, who took in only one boarder for the sake of a little extra money and maybe also for a little extra company now that their children had all moved away. Big elms and maples all around. A lawn out front that he mowed for them some-times. A big garden that he used to help Bob weed in the evening, talking away about this and that, Bob asking him sometimes about the war and him telling the usual, well-sanitized lies.

In the morning, he washed and shaved in an upstairs bathroom that faced east and in the morning was always filled with light. Then dressed up in a suit and tie the way he used to be the year he went to high school, he walked up through town to the woodworking factory and an office of his own, where he worked at accounts at a desk with a little sign with his name on it. Mr. John Maclean. A window looked out over the back lumber yard towards the hills across the river, where he never went now and intended never to go again ever, far away here from the farm and the dirt.

"You miserable, old bastard, what do you know about anything?"

"You speak to me like that? You speak to me like that! God will smite you!"

"God doesn't give a shit."

"God will smite."

A scrawny fist shaking with rage. Mother cowering in a chair at the kitchen table. Then upstairs, throwing his things into an old knapsack, down the stairs and out, down the road and away, the river whispering among the bushes on the bank, the town on the far side fixed on its hills in the summer heat. And the sense gathering, as he crossed the bridge, of freedom at last and life after all in spite of everything.

But even then there were times when all of a sudden that good world with its nice room and its garden and his good job seemed unreal—a kind of curtain on which all these

things were just a painted show, like a curtain he once saw in
a theatre in London with a country scene on it which disappeared when a light was turned on, so that you saw behind it
a different scene with real people. Once, walking back from
work on a rainy afternoon that was already getting dark in
the damp cold of November, he saw a man coming up the
hill towards him. For a few seconds, terrified, he took him to
be Sergeant Death, but when he got close, he turned out to
be a harmless little man who worked in a clothing store on
Main Street.

I'm sorry, John, but there just ain't the work. I got to let
half the boys in the shop and the yard go too. Mary's going
to keep the books, and her mother's going to come in to
look after the kids. If things pick up again, you'll have your
job back the very first day I can afford it. I'm sorry, John.
There just ain't the work any more. It's a bad time.

Old vets, like himself, on street corners coming to see that
in the years they had been away the ones who had stayed
home, the smart ones, light-footed, had been making money
and getting ahead, and they, the heroes, the stupid ones, were
never going to catch up.

Well, it's over now, the fat little man at the employment
bureau said, and the world has to go on, don't it? What did
you say your name was? Yes. Yes. Angus Maclean's son. A
little gas. Yes. We'll see. Yes. Yes.

He peed as quietly as he could against the side of the bowl
so as not to be heard and buttoned up and stood looking
out the window again at the yard. Surrounded by these

reminders of long-vanished possibility, he found the face of Claudine Swann taking shape in his imagination. It had been a long time since she had last risen to haunt him, of all his memories the most carefully buried in the spacious graveyard of the past.

Mrs. Claudine Swann, as she was generally called, was the widow of Private Eldon Swann. Because of his fascination with pipes and kilts and all things Scottish, Eldon Swann had left George County and enlisted in the North Nova Scotia Highlanders, and one weekend in 1916, when he was on leave in Halifax, he went to a dance and met Claudine MacCrae. A month later they were married, and a month after that he was on a ship to France.

For some reason, Claudine moved to Wakefield to await his return. But Private Eldon Swann did not return. He was killed a few days before the Armistice. With the prospect of peace so close, he got careless maybe, or maybe some general back in his chateau decided to use his last chance to improve his record by capturing another few acres of mud.

When she first came to Wakefield, Claudine lived for a while with her in-laws, but they didn't get on, and she moved to a small apartment over a store off Main Street. She was still living there when, like Private Eldon Swann, Maclean met her at a dance.

They were both a little tight. She had come with another couple, an ex-soldier and his girlfriend. Maclean knew the ex-soldier a little, and they fell into talk. After a while, he had a dance with Claudine, then another, and soon found himself part of a foursome.

In spite of the gas, he was still a good-looking man in those days, he still had his job at the woodworking factory,

and he was well aware of the popular view that a man such
as himself should be in search of a wife. Except at a respectful distance, he had never had anything to do with a woman
since he went to the war. The whores of England had not
attracted him, the whores of France still less, and no other
possible relationship had ever come his way. There were now
plenty of unattached women around, thanks to the war, but
he didn't feel the impulse to pursue them. When asked, as
he sometimes was, about his single state, he served up the
stock reply that he had not yet met the right girl.

After the dance, he walked Claudine to the building
where her apartment was. It was after midnight, and the
streets were deserted. Standing in the door way, she kissed
him goodnight and pressed his hand.

Claudine Swann was small with thick, reddish-brown
hair, brown eyes, and a sharp foxlike face. She wasn't par-
ticularly pretty, but she had a good deal of whatever it is
that can make a woman attractive regardless of her looks.
Working away at his desk, Maclean found himself thinking
about her, and half way through the following week, he went
around to the store where she worked and asked her to the
next Saturday's dance. After that, they began going out to
dances, movies, the races, band concerts. One night she took
him by the hand and led him upstairs.

Although he always went back to his own room to sleep
(How would he have explained an all-night absence to Bob
and Clara? How long would it have been before the talk
started? How long before his boss at the woodworking
factory decided to have a "word" with him?), over the next
couple of months, her apartment took on some of the quali-
ties of home.

She didn't have much, and much of what she had was second-hand or third- or fourth-hand. Well-worn furniture, well-chipped dishes, well-dented pots and pans, an unmatching assortment of cheap "silverware." The oilcloth on the floor had been worn down in places almost to the boards underneath. The wallpaper was overlain by a layer of dirt the colour of weak tea and in places had begun to peel. One of the windows was cracked. (Even after a quarter of a century, he could still remember the precise location and shape of every one of these disfigurations.)

Within this context of neglect and decay, Claudine had made things as cheerful as she could with colourful curtains and calendars and pictures from rummage sales of far, imaginary places.

She never spoke of Eldon Swann, and once he realized she didn't want to, he never spoke of him either. Now and then she let drop remarks that suggested other dark memories, but she volunteered nothing more about them, and he didn't pry. Since she knew that he had parents on the other side of the river whom he never visited, he told her about them one night in a monologue that lasted almost the whole evening. Then that too was consigned to silence. Sometimes she asked him about the war, and he told her whatever she wanted to know, wondering whether what she was asking about might not be Private Eldon Swann and what his dying might have been like. She never said what had happened to him. Perhaps she didn't know.

For a while, what they did talk about were mostly things of no deep importance—her job, his job, the things they had done (or not done), the people they met, the goings-on of the town—sometimes, though not often, the goings-on in the great world that neither of them wanted anything more to do with.

She didn't have a lot of schooling. Grade Eight, she said, in a country school in Cape Breton. Coming across unexpected abysses of ignorance, he sometimes wondered if she had even less schooling than that and was lying to him because she was intimidated by his year and a half of high school with its Shakespeare and French and Latin. But although she might not have been well-educated, she was clever and alert and knew far more about life—meaning the lives of men and women—than he had ever had a chance to know.

Among the many things they didn't talk about was the future, which was to say, their future. She didn't talk about it, he suspected, because she was afraid. He didn't talk about it, he told himself, because for the moment the present was enough.

Sometime in the next few weeks, the right moment would come when they would talk. But before that moment came, there came the morning when he went to the factory and found out that he had lost his job.

He could still have afforded his room on his pension and the money he had saved, but the very next week, he moved out and into a one-room apartment in an old, wooden tenement building beside the creek, a great rabbit-warren of a place full of poor people, mostly Catholic Irish, with broods of sad, dirty children.

"Why?" Claudine shouted at him. "Why for Christ's sake? Tell me why?"

"It's all I can afford."

"Bullshit. And anyway you can live here."

"No."

"Why not? Why in Christ's name not?"

Why not?

As the money he had saved began to run out, he found a job helping to dig a basement, another chopping the winter's firewood for a store.

He began to drink more, and she drank along with him although never so much. Some nights now, he did stay all night, waking in the morning in the stale heat of the apartment with an aching head and a dead weight in his stomach.

This went on for weeks. Sometimes they fought, usually over nothing of any importance. Mostly they merely wallowed in a kind of dank despair which gathered at first in him but soon generated a counterpart in her. They hardly went anywhere any more, and there were times when they sat all evening at her kitchen table and hardly said a word. He brooded about his lost job, his lost education, the war. He didn't know what she brooded about, apart perhaps from her lost husband. As was her way, she never said.

One day in early fall, she told him she was going to visit her sister in Halifax. A week after she left, he got a letter saying she wasn't coming back. It said hardly more than that she saw no future for them and that it seemed to her they would do better without each other.

The letter was postmarked Halifax. It had no return address, but the little she had told him about her people was still enough that he knew he could get in touch with her if he wanted to. Maybe she knew that too. Maybe it was all a kind of test.

For months, he carried the letter around in his billfold.

One of the boys from the army lived in Halifax, and he could easily have written him and given him the information he would need to locate Claudine. Twice he sat down and began to write, but before he had finished, something, he hardly knew what, came between him and his intent.

Then one night, very drunk, going through his billfold in a futile search for money, he came across Claudine's letter and tore it up and threw the pieces away.

Why? In Christ's name, why? Was there lurking somewhere some kind of insane pride, without sense or purpose, that would not let him consent to be the husband of this simple, good woman? Had the wounds he had suffered finally rendered him unfit for active service in the world?

He gave his battered face a final look in Alice's mirror, then turned away and went out into the hall. A doorway led to the living room in the old part of the house, a room with everything needed for a comfortable evening at home. Off in one corner, a collection of photographs was arranged on a big oak table.

He slid through the doorway and crept like a thief across the room. Some of the photographs were recent, some from long ago. A photograph of Alice and Mitch in front of the house all dressed up for some occasion. A photograph of Alice's daughters and their husbands and children. The wedding photograph of Mother and Father. Mother, small and elegant, looking wistful, as if foreseeing the future, the way people in photographs sometimes do. Father drawn up stern, scowling into the camera so that God would not think that he really cared for such vanity as this. A studio photograph of Alice aged eighteen or so, looking very pretty in a white dress with a white ribbon in her hair. A photograph of the children and their teachers in front of the old school across the river. Himself, Alice, Harry. Elsie Skadget, big and awkward, smiling her big smile over the heads of shyer, smaller kids.

Apart from the school picture, there were no photographs of him. His father would have destroyed them all. Just as years before he had destroyed all the photographs of his mother's people, the Somervilles. Once when he had asked his mother why his father had said that her father was some kind of a bad man, she had said that her father wasn't a bad man but that Father didn't like him, that was all. And the reason Father didn't like him, it turned out a long time later when Maclean was old enough to understand such things, was that her father had been a man who could play the piano and had taken part in plays and operettas and, more sinful even than that, had been far better off than Angus Maclean. He hated all the Somervilles, and once when his mother had sneaked off to see one of her sisters who was ill, he had locked her in the pantry and wouldn't let her out. Later, when the sister died, he wouldn't let her go to the funeral, and she sat outside on the bench beside the kitchen door, listening to the bell of the Anglican Church tolling on the far side of the river.

He looked back at the studio photograph of Alice. How pretty she was! If somehow he had never seen her after that photograph was taken—if, for example, she had moved away while he was at the war and then, now, moved back, looking the way she now looked, and he had met her on the street, he wouldn't have known her. It was as if there was another person altogether still living somewhere there in the past who had nothing to do with the fat, sweating old woman with her straggly hair who was in the kitchen making cookies. Or as if maybe, somewhere along some other branch of the road of time, there was an Alice this age, but not this Alice—an Alice who had been let go to high school and had married Harry Noles, who had not gone to the war, not been blown to pieces at Festubert. And another John Maclean too who had not gone to the war either because he had finished high school and had better things to do with his life than join the army and fight for the god-damned English.

He became aware that Alice was standing in the doorway behind him, wondering no doubt what had been taking him so long, not knowing what journeys, backward and sideways, he had been making through the tangle of life.

"I've been looking at the old pictures here," he said.

She came and stood beside him, silently, then picked up the wedding photograph.

"Tomorrow's the day father died," she said. "Mother's birthday. It was so hot that day."

She stared out the window, looking beyond the pots of geraniums on the window sill and the fir trees on the other side of the road, down the years into the upstairs room where their father lay.

His office job at the woodworking factory was long gone by then, along with all the fine speeches about a country fit for heroes, and he had been through a succession of menial, short-term jobs, interspersed by a good many times when he had no job at all. That morning, when the boy from across the river came to tell him that his father was dead, he was piling lumber as a day labourer at the woodworking factory whose books he had once kept.

He got his pay from the office and walked across the bridge against the flow of wagons and trucks on their way to town. Alice was right. It was hot, the sun beating down out of a cloudless sky, even the asphalt on the bridge getting soft underfoot.

It was the first time he had been in the house in years, the first time he had been in his father's bedroom ever. His father lay on his back, his face skeletal and white, his mouth half open, his hand lying on the quilts, the fingers curled up like claws.

He had seen too many dead to be bothered by one more, and he could think of nothing to make him sorrowful for this one. From all those years, he could not remember one act of kindness or generosity, no matter how small, that this man had ever performed for anybody.

But his mother and Alice were weeping.

"You never made it up," Alice said.

"No. And neither would he unless I wanted to go back there and work for him for nothing."

"Well," Alice said.

She turned away from the table, abruptly, and he sensed her irritation.

"My cookies are gonna be burnin' up," she said.

She went out, and he followed her, and sat down again at the table, wondering whether he should not now get away, but held there by some need or other—perhaps some such craziness as a notion that just by talking to Alice, he could take them back to that fork in the road of time where they could make the turn towards the lives they ought to have had.

He watched her pull the cookie sheet with the peanut

butter cookies out of the oven and replace it with another.

"There wasn't any need for him to take you out of school," he said, abruptly, without having made any decision that he was going to say it, the craziness taking him over as if he were a ventriloquist's dummy. "You could have gone to high school and done just fine."

"Mamma needed the help. You know that."

"No, she didn't. It was him. He wanted everyone to be as ignorant as he was, sitting around with his god-damned Bible laying down the law as if he were God himself."

"That's no way to talk about him. Anyway it was a long time ago."

She unloaded the cookie sheet and went back to the frosting in the double boiler.

"There wasn't any need for him to take me out of school either," Maclean said.

"They needed you too. On the farm."

"For six months, there wasn't anything I couldn't do in two hours after school. The rest of the year he could have hired somebody."

"I don't suppose he had the money."

"He had all of Mamma's money that she got from her father. And that wasn't all. Uncle Andrew told Mamma that he would pay to hire a man so I could stay in school."

Alice stopped stirring.

"Who told you that?"

"Aunt Elizabeth. After the war. After Andrew died. She told me herself. She said that Andrew got Mamma to tell him, and he wouldn't hear of it. Andrew even went over himself, and Father ordered him out of the house. It didn't have anything to do with money."

"I never heard that. Anyway, you still got a good job when you left the farm."

"It didn't last long."

Alice carried the top of a double boiler over to the table and began frosting a cake that had been sitting there under a glass cover.

"You could have got another job if you'd tried," she said. "The trouble with you is that you always thought you were too good for an ordinary job."

She looked at him over her shoulder, closely again, at the bruise on his forehead, and all over him, clothes, hands, everything. He could see that she was beginning to simmer, and he could feel the conversation sliding relentlessly towards familiar ground. He knew for sure that the time had come when he should get up and leave, but he didn't.

"I worked at lots of ordinary jobs. Try peeling pulp sometime."

"You worked at ordinary jobs just long enough to get yourself some money to get drunk on. You'd have been better off if they hadn't given you no pension at all. Then maybe you'd have had to get yourself some kind of steady job and stick to it or starve. You could still get some kind of light work like carpenter work and get some kind of decent wage and live a decent life."

"There isn't any decent life," he said.

"What's that supposed to mean?"

"Nothing," he said. "Nothing."

"You can't even talk sense," she said, and she went back to frosting her cake, scraping the frosting out of the bowl, spreading it on the cake with jerky, furious little movements, her lips pursed tight.

He sat with his elbows on the table and looked at her. Her
fat, corpse-white legs with their great blotches and wrig-
gling varicose veins. Her fat, corpse-white arms. Her fat
neck with a fold and a ring where it met the fat of her back.
The straggly hair like a mop someone had stood up in a
corner. The sweat spreading down the back of her dress. The
whole, great shapeless hulk of her hunched over the table. If
anything, she looked worse than he did.

I wandered lonely as a cloud that floats on high o'er vales
and hills.

"You should have married Harry Noles," he said.

"What?" she said. "What? I didn't hear."

"I said you should have married Harry Noles. You should
just have walked out."

"Harry was killed in the war, you know that. What are you
talkin' about?"

"I mean before the war. You let Father drive him out. You
just gave in. You should have walked out and lived your own
life."

"I told you. They needed the help, him and Mamma."

"Bullshit."

"Don't you talk like that in my house. And what's the
sense of bringin' all this stuff up after all these years?"

"You could have walked out and gone to Uncle Andrew's
place and gone to high school and married Harry and had a
good life."

"I do have a good life. Mitch is a good man. I have nice
children. And grandchildren. You ain't got no right to talk
against Mitch. We ain't never wanted for anything we needed. Not never. Why do you come here and bring all this
up again. There ain't no sense to it. It just makes me upset,

and then my heart goes funny. The doctor said I shouldn't get myself upset over things. What's the sense of all this? What's the sense?"

"There isn't any sense."

"Look at you. With your face all bruised up, scroungin' around the streets and alleys and fightin' and gettin' yourself put in jail and livin' like some kind of wild animal. Mitch is worth ten of you."

It always ended up like this. What had he come here for? The Black Rock. The fighting. The old school. The dying maple with its banner of flame. But earlier too. Even that morning. Someone, something, sneaking past the sentries he had posted, had thrown wide the gates of memory.

Alice started to cry.

"Why do you come here?" she wailed.

He walked as fast as he could down the gravel road. A quarter of a mile from Alice's place, it passed through another little patch of woods, then emerged onto a more civilized road that ran above the creek and back to the centre of town. The little valley the creek ran through broadened out here into a wide stretch of interval land, hot now in the sun, with yellow hayfields and fringes of trees along the creek and the little purdues that cut into the flat land. Off towards the far side of the valley, a hay wagon drawn by two horses was moving slowly away, and just below him two boys were fishing in a little square-nosed punt.

Once when he was in hospital in England before they decided he was no longer healthy enough to be killed, some English ladies, one of the groups that turned up to do something for the boys, took a dozen of them to a great house in the country. It was summer and fine for a change, and they all went bouncing along in a pair of funny, tall little buses with wooden sides.

In one of the rooms of the house, there was an enormous painting of a countryside with a little stream and great oak trees and cattle wading and drinking and a wagon just making its way down to a ford in the stream and flat distances with fences and trees disappearing in a haze of sunlight. While the others were touring the house, he sat on a fancy sofa and looked and looked, imagining himself stepping into the picture and wandering off across those fields.

After a while one of the ladies who had brought them, a little gray-haired lady dressed all in black, came up to him and asked, "Feeling a little tired, Private Maclean?"

"Yes," he said. "A little."

She stood looking at the picture, and then as if reading his thought she said, "It's beautiful, isn't it. It makes you want to walk away from all this and never come back."

9

"Did you know," Henry said, "that in fifteen years every cell in your body dies and a new cell gets put in its place?"

"No," Maclean said. "No, I didn't know that."

"That's right," Henry said. "There ain't one cell in your body that was there fifteen years ago."

"Is that so?" Maclean said. "Well, well."

"It makes you wonder what goes on makin' you the same person, don't it?" Henry said. "I guess it must be the soul."

"And what if you don't have any soul?" Maclean asked.

"You have to have a soul," Henry said. "It just stands to reason."

"Like God."

"That's right. Like God."

Not five o'clock yet and the shadows from the elm trees behind the house were already across the road and into the grass on the other side. The summer was dying. After many a summer dies the swan. Man comes and tills the fields and where is he? Alfred Lloyd Tennyson, one of the class dumbbells said. Everybody laughed. Not Lloyd, Mr. Dingley, Mr. Raymond said. Lord. Alfred, Lord Tennyson. Queen Victoria made him a Lord because he was a great poet.

"The woods decay, the woods decay and fall," Maclean said.

"Poetry?" Henry asked.

"Yes," Maclean said.

"You still read poetry," Henry said. "That's wonderful."

"It was in an old school reader."

"I was never any good at poetry," Henry said. "Most of the time I just couldn't make any sense out of it."

"It don't matter," Maclean said. "It'll put the right words in your head sometimes, but it don't change anything much."

He had a pain in his shoulder and a general sense of aches all over. The fight at the Black Rock had hurt him worse than he thought. But there was always a pain somewhere, and he got so used to it that if he didn't have one somewhere he would wonder what was wrong with him.

After supper, he would go up town and get the present and take it up to his mother and come back and go to bed and have a good sleep and tomorrow, he would take it easy all day just sitting out here watching the clouds and the river go by and listening to Henry telling him about mankind and the history of the world. The fishhawk was back, circling high up above the river, slowly without effort, tipping a wing, sliding away, riding up again. Soon, he would be going south to wherever they went for the winter. The woods decay, the woods decay and fall.

Miss Audrey Sweet came out, and Henry got up and gave her his wicker chair and moved over and sat on the wooden bench along the end of the verandah. She had changed out of her work clothes into a bright print dress, and she had got her wiry hair combed into some kind of order and pinned a little, flat felt hat to the top of it and put on some rouge and perfume. On Saturday night, she always went to the service at the Salvation Army chapel.

She looked at the river and the hills and the sky with its white clouds and the fishhawk. Her pale blue eyes behind her glasses were bright the way a child's are bright, and she smiled as she took in one by one these wonders of the afternoon.

"Now isn't this all just beautiful," she said.

She was always cheerful. But she wasn't cheerful the way Henry was cheerful. Henry was cheerful because it was his nature. Miss Audrey was cheerful because she couldn't afford to let herself not be. Once in the middle of the night, Maclean had gone downstairs to the bathroom because someone was in the one upstairs. As he went by her room, he noticed that the door was ajar and in the light from the outside he could just make out the shape of her kneeling there in the darkness beside her bed. He wondered about her getting up to pray that time of night, but as he broke step just for a second passing the door, he could hear that she wasn't praying but sobbing.

"God's in his heaven," Maclean said. "All's right with the world."

"That's just the truth, Mr. Maclean," Miss Audrey said.

In her room, Mrs. Fraser was lying looking up at the ceiling. Maclean slipped past and unlocked his door and stepped quietly inside and closed the door behind him. He sat down on his bed, tired and still conscious of the pain in his shoulder. He took out his change purse and poured the five remaining coins out into his palm. A dime with the new king on it, a nickel and three pennies with old King George V, whom he had seen once a long way off when he came to Salisbury to review the old First Division. Enough for a pack of tailor-made Turrets and a package of tobacco. And he could keep back twenty-five of the seventy-five he had hidden.

He got up and quietly pulled out the drawer of his dresser and fished out the brown envelope. He took out the ration book with his liquor coupons and looked into the bottom of the envelope.

There was nothing there.

He tried to think. Sometimes he forgot things. Sometimes he thought he had done things that he hadn't done. Or found that he had done things that he didn't remember doing. But he remembered the beer bottles and working for Jim and getting the extra fifty cents and coming back with it all, not being anywhere that anybody could have picked it off him. He had put it there and no doubt, and someone had got into his room and stolen it. He felt his rage building and told himself that he had to keep calm and think.

Who? Who could have got in? The door was locked. But Drusilla's fat daughters came in to clean. They would have all the time in the world to search the room. Or Walter. Any old skeleton key would open that lock. Walter didn't work on Saturday afternoons. He could have slipped in and searched. There weren't many places in a room like this where you could hide things, and now he saw that it had been stupid to put money in a place like that. Anyone searching the room would think almost first thing of looking under the drawers. He should have known that. Stupid. He should have given the money to Henry to keep for him.

As he thought about it, he realized the girls wouldn't have dared. They would be too afraid of Drusilla. The boys down the hall wouldn't do it. And not Henry, not ever, not if he were starving to death. It had to be Walter Haynes. God damn him, the pig-faced son of a whore.

He found himself walking up and down the room, back and forth between the window and the door like a crazy man. Like the crazy men in the hospital back of Ypres. He was even talking out loud to himself. Shovels, one man kept saying as he stormed back and forth, ten paces one way, ten paces the other, but staring ahead all the time with a far look in his eyes, as if he was walking down a long, straight road towards some distant goal. Shovels. Shovels. Shovels.

"You not feelin' good," Henry asked.

"No," Maclean said. "Fine. Fine."

He looked at the baked beans on his plate. Beans with thick slices of fresh porkside. And brown bread. Maclean liked beans and brown bread, especially the bread. But his appetite was gone.

The MacDonald boys weren't eating much either. They'd had all afternoon to think about Alex getting his call, and they weren't saying anything, and nobody liked to ask them anything. Nobody, that is, except Walter.

"So when d'ya go off to Fredericton," he asked Alex.

"Wednesday," Alex said. "Next Wednesday."

"You goin' too then?" Walter asked Doug.

"I don't know," Doug said. "I ain't really decided."

Anyone who wasn't as chicken-brained as Walter could see that Alex didn't want to go off by himself and that Doug didn't want to go, not yet anyway, and that to haul it up at the supper table in front of everybody was putting Doug on the spot.

Maclean had been watching Walter, and whenever his

eyes met Walter's, Walter looked away, not too fast, but he always looked away. It was him who took the money. No doubt about it. If he knew he could get away with it, Maclean could have killed him.

Some of the boys did that once in France. His name was Blanstock. A replacement. By that time, most of them were replacements. From somewere in northern Ontario. He stole. Stuff people had got from home, anything. And he didn't even pretend not to because he felt sure he could beat the hell out of anybody in the company who tried to take him on. He even stole a boy's boots because his had got a cut in one of them. Prove it, Blanstock said. Prove it. And he was all ready to beat the boy up. Harper. That was the boy's name. He'd only just got there, and he was killed a couple of weeks later by a sniper, still wearing the old boot with the cut in it that Blanstock had left him.

Blanstock never got it into his head that this wasn't any northern Ontario lumber camp. So one night when the shells were coming down in one's and two's just to make life miserable, he was in a party going back through a communication trench, and the boys let him get around a corner into the next leg of the trench by himself and took the pin out and rolled a grenade after him. And what with the shelling, nobody knew the difference. Or pretended they didn't anyway.

It was funny, Maclean thought, how the same people keep re-appearing over and over again. Blanstock. Willie. This son of a whore Haynes. As if God, or nature, or whoever, didn't have much imagination when it came to making people instead of birds and animals.

He looked at the MacDonald boys and wondered what he should say to Doug, if he were going to say anything—which he wasn't. Stay out of it? Or stick with your pal? He would go. He was that sort. And they would both get themselves killed because they were that sort. And that's why wars go on getting fought. Because the world is full of people like the MacDonald boys, who go because they're dumb and stick it out because they don't want to let down their pals. Somewhere up there, well out of danger in their offices and clubs, well above the mud, the blood, and the shit, there were people who understood that.

Maclean hiked once more down the road towards town. There was still sunlight on the tops of the hills, but the valley bottom was in shadow, and in eastward facing windows a few lights were coming on. A radio was playing cowboy music somewhere and somewhere someone was playing "Carry Me Back to Old Virginny" on a piano.

Half way to the railroad bridge, he swung off the road up a steep little street to the tracks and then along between the main line and a siding, his boots grinding and slithering in the loose clinkers. His mind was still racing, and his heart too. Someday it would get him. The gas has weakened your heart, the doctor said to him from on high, and it has to work harder because your lungs are bad. Light work would be best. A store maybe. Perhaps you know somebody.

As he walked, keeping a lookout for bottles, his eyes took in the familiar scene. Weathered, gray loading sheds with rusting metal signs for chicken feed and flour. Weeds. Clinkers. Broken glass. An old newspaper. Lying curled up between the rails of the siding, a freshly dead rat that must have got poisoned in one of the feed sheds and made it that far in its search for water before the poison got to it. Sparrows hopping around in the clinkers looking for bits of dropped grain. Along the roof trees of the sheds, lines of well-fed pigeons fluttering and fussing. Wurble. Wurble. Wurble. No bottles. And none of the boys either. Too early. Too light. The whole place deserted except for himself and the pigeons and the sparrows and the dead rat.

Carefully, down the middle between the rails, placing one foot deliberately after the other, skipping one tie each time, he made his way out onto the railway bridge, looking down now and then in spite of himself between the ties to where the water swirled and eddied among the rocks, spreading out, finding its way again after pouring through the sluice gates of the little dam the town had built to keep the water level up in the hot summer months. Above the dam, the water was as smooth as a mirror, reflecting the red light of the declining sun, and on the bridge by the square, men were leaning on the rails talking while the steady flow of Saturday night traffic moved back and forth behind them.

He glanced ahead. He had a couple of dozen more ties to go before he reached the centre span of the bridge with its waist-high steel trusses. The unprotected sheer drop off the sides of the two end spans always made him nervous, as if somehow it had the power to call to some hidden assassin inside himself who would draw him over to the edge and down. As he approached the centre span, he began counting down what he guessed to be the remaining ties. Sixteen. Fourteen. Twelve.

Suddenly, without so much as a preliminary flutter, a flock

of pigeons burst upwards from their perches underneath the bridge and wheeled around him, their wings almost brushing his face. He threw up one arm, and his heel came down in the space between the ties. He fought to keep his balance, found it, and at the same instant heard the ticking of the rails that signaled an approaching train. He looked up and saw the smoke billowing up above the coal sheds along the curve off the end of the bridge. The train whistled, sounding almost on top of him already. It would have whistled twice already for crossings further up, and he hadn't heard either one, still lost in his furious calculations about how to replace his stolen money.

That's how it always happened, one day when they were thinking about something else and their head stayed up at a gap between the sandbags and the sniper was waiting with the gap in his sights, supernaturally alert and infinitely patient.

He stood frozen. He didn't have time to get back off the bridge before the train got to him. All he could do was try to make the centre span. Fighting his panic, still keeping to the middle between the rails away from the drop over the side, trying to put his feet down solidly on the ties, taking just one at a time now, short and quick, he made his way. Eight. Seven. Six. Jesus. The engine appeared around the end of the coal shed, coming fast. It blew again, and the sound nearly took him off his feet. He reached the centre span and got out from between the rails, imagining himself at the last second catching his foot sideways between the ties and being held there. He wouldn't have been the first person to have been killed on that bridge, taking a short cut to town and eternity or oblivion or wherever.

He took hold of the steel plating of the truss and edged his way a little further along. He had made six more feet before the engine came up to him and blew again, a long blast, full-whistle, that kept up as the engine passed, engulfing him in escaping steam and a tornado of sound, the whistle, the pounding wheels, the thunder and hiss of the driving pistons. His head knew that he was safe, as safe as if he were a mile away, but his body didn't know that. His body had memories, and he was shivering like an animal under the battering weight of the noise.

"Jesus. Jesus," the boy beside him kept shouting. "Make them stop. Make them stop."

"Keep down, you god-damned fool! Keep down!"

He looked up, at the water falling through the sluice gates silently, at the traffic going back and forth on the other bridge silently, at the people leaning calmly on the rails talking to each other, as if they were in another world from him here bent over the edge of the truss, terrified, shivering, the wheels pounding relentlessly beside him, shaking the bridge under his feet.

The earth shook. The earth shook and erupted and stank of explosive, and the almost naked body of a man, spilling blood and guts, its legs blown to tatters, came tumbling end over end down over the parados.

He looked across his shoulder and saw that there were only three more cars and the caboose. He let his breath flow out and watched them come with the kind of limp indifference that was always the first feeling when the terror was over. As the caboose passed, the conductor of the train in his little box on top looked down at him without any change of expression or any sign to him at all, as if he were nothing more than a dead rat or a piece of dog shit beside the track.

Does God look down on all this? God is dead. A shell full of mustard gas got him while he was having a glass of wine and a loaf of bread beside the Menin Road. It was all in the division paper last week. The Maple Leaf Rag. Didn't you read it? When you've been triaged, Maclean, and you're lying on your back looking up at the ceiling of the dead tent, you won't be so god-damned smart.

He straightened up. Overhead against the fading blue of the evening sky, the pigeons were wheeling and swooping. At the top of Main Street, the clock began striking seven.

He sat on the corner of the porch of the Farmer's Store to get his wind back, not giving a damn about the farmers who stood around the door, their talk momentarily stilled as they looked at him in their squint-eyed, farmerly way. Fuck them. He wasn't drunk. He had never been more sober in his life. But his ears were ringing, and there was a dull, regular throbbing in his head as if a second heart were beating in there.

After the first war ended and before the second one started, they used to call him in every year or so for a medical examination. They told him it was to look after his health. More likely, they were looking for some excess of well-being that would give them an excuse for stopping his pension. The last few times he went, they told him he had high blood pressure. Strokes, they said. Heart attacks. Don't excite yourself, they said. I used up all my excitement a long time ago, he said.

He tried to think through some plan of what to do. Jim's stable would still be open. He could go back and tell him what happened to his money and ask him for more, just this once, maybe as a loan or an advance on another morning's work, and Jim would look at him with his head cocked to one side the way he did, and he would give him the money, but he wouldn't for one second believe the money had been stolen, and he would never give him money again nor even let him go through the make-believe of earning it. No, he thought, not worth it.

He crossed the street into an alley that brought him out onto Main Street.

The sidewalks were full. More people than ever. Country people, their business done, standing around talking and looking. Town people shopping for a few more things for Sunday dinner. Young bucks sitting with their elbows out the windows of cars, watching the girls. Girls parading in two's and three's, acting indifferent but waiting for the right ones to ask them to a dance somewhere. Soldiers from the armoury, Zombies mostly. Other soldiers home on leave sporting their little GS badges for the girls. A few Americans, smooth and smug, looking like bellboys in their serge uniforms, giving the Canadians a wide berth.

Half way down the hill, the Salvation Army band was playing away, a little circle of a dozen brass instruments with tambourine and big bass drum, serenading with the word of the Lord. Are you washed in the blood of the Lamb? Rattle Rattle Boom Boom. Are you washed in the blood of the Lamb? Onward, Joe Soap's Army. Marching along singing, a little column of fox-faced Cockneys. Until a few weeks before, they would never have fired a rifle in their lives, and they still couldn't hit the broad side of a barn with it. Not that it was going to make much difference. Rattle Rattle Boom Boom.

He threaded his way up the street. The liquor store was closed and dark, and as he passed, he saw himself reflected in the window, shabby and insubstantial among the crowd of people, insubstantial also, as if they were all already ghosts and this was already the long-dead past it would one day become.

At the top of the hill, he crossed the street from the post office and hoisted himself backwards up onto the concrete retaining wall of the lawn in front of the library and sat leaning forward, his elbows on his knees. Across Main Street a trickle of people still passed in and out of the post office. Behind him, two middle-aged women descended the steps of the library, turned, and passed him with averted eyes, one of them carrying cradled in her arms a copy of *Gone with the Wind*, the title much faded on the scuffed spine. I have forgot much, Cynara! gone with the wind. Not so.

He sat on one side, Cynthia on the other, of the long oak table with its piles of magazines lined neatly down the centre. *The National Geographic. The Illustrated London News. Punch. The Saturday Evening Post.* In the middle of the table, a small sign said SILENCE. A late afternoon in late winter, an afternoon not long before the crash. They were supposed to be looking up information on Samuel Taylor Coleridge's "The Rime of the Ancient Mariner" for Mr. Raymond's class the next day, and they were pretending to consult the questions in their notebooks. She was a tall, angular girl with very dark hair, very dark eyes, not pretty but good-looking in her own way all the same, a quiet girl, a reader.

Twice he had sneaked away to go to the Anglican Church with her and sat near the back in the pews that were nobody's in particular. His mother's relatives, Anglicans all, sat in their particular pews near the front. Morning sunlight falling through the stained glass windows. Rich woodwork. Leather-bound prayer books. The slow, prescribed ritual. Mr. Raymond in his choir robes marching solemnly in procession behind the cross.

You men there! You men there! What are you doing in this place? Get out where you belong. This is not a public house.

She was one of the students standing in the hall the day he had gone back to get his books. He had pretended not to notice her. Afterwards, before he went overseas, he saw her sometimes on the street, but always in time to turn off some other way. Then, while he was overseas, she married and moved away.

From an alley beside the town hall, Jimmy McIninch stepped out onto the street and looked up and down as if he were all ready to slip back into the alley, like a groundhog on top of a rock pile checking a field for foxes or dogs. Except that Jimmy looked more like a fox than a groundhog. He caught sight of Maclean and sidled across the street.

"So what's up?" he asked when he had got himself up onto the wall.

"Nothing," Maclean said. "Nothing much."

"You ain't seen Willie Campbell or Junior Tedley?"

"No," Maclean said.

"Junior's been tellin' everybody that the five of us ganged up on Willie and that Willie's gonna find us one by one and beat the shit out of us."

"Fuck him," Maclean said.

"Better stay out of his way, all the same."

"I never touched the son of a whore," Maclean said. "If you see Junior again, tell him that if Willie lays a finger on any of us, we'll set Ginger on him, and this time we won't pull him off."

"Well," Jimmy said, "it's a hard, old world, now ain't it?"

"It's that," Maclean said. "Truth is, I'm in sort of a fix. I need a quarter bad. Fifty cents if I could get it."

"I ain't got a thing," Jimmy said. "Just a dime, that's all. What d'ya need it for?"

Maclean hesitated.

"My mother's birthday tomorrow," he said, "and I always get her something. I worked at Jim Gartley's this morning and made some money, but somebody stole it down at the house. Every cent I earned."

"Jesus," Jimmy said. "That's terrible. Now who'd do a thing like that?"

"I think I know, but I'd rather not say."

"Bill Kayton might help ya out," Jimmy said. "But I ain't seen him since this afternoon. What about Leveret? He usually has sumpin' in his pocket even when he says he don't."

"Probably he does," Maclean said. "But he's never very quick to part with it."

"True," Jimmy said. "But it don't do no harm to ask. I think he goes to the Legion Saturday nights and plays cards and sets around."

"I used to see him there," Maclean said. "But I don't go there much lately."

He looked up at the town clock. A quarter to eight. He thought about Leveret and the Legion Hall.

Shit, he said to himself.

10

The lounge in the Legion Hall was almost full, a low uproar of talk broken into every few seconds by outbursts of laughter. The old guys telling each other lies about the war. Some soldiers home on leave. A few Zombies from the garrison in the armoury. They weren't too popular with some people, and there had been talk about throwing them out, but no one had got up to doing it yet. And some of the boys even said, good for them, what fucking good did going over there ever do for us.

As he stood near the door looking around for Leveret, he could see the eyes turning towards him, just a pair or two at first, then more turning to see what the others had found to look at. Fuck them, he thought, I've got as much right to be here as anybody and more than most.

Leveret was sitting on the far side of the room with an old artilleryman named Pickle. ("Must have killed all kinds of Germans, but I never seen one 'til the war was almost over and this big bunch of prisoners come marchin' by us one day.") Leveret was one of the last to notice Maclean, and when he did, he nodded to him in his grandest manner like the mayor acknowledging a deferential tip of the cap from the town dog-catcher. The Black Rock was one thing, but this here was another.

Maclean nodded back, not too much, not too little, a circumspect kind of nod that he could move either way from.

He straightened himself up and made his way along the side of the room to the counter, trying to look like a man who came in every day. He hated to do it, but he put down the money for a glass of Moosehead. He didn't like beer much, but it was the cheapest thing he could buy, and it would be his ticket to sitting down with Leveret and Pickle without having them worry first thing that he had come to bum the price of a drink.

Leveret and Pickle both had glasses of whiskey. Bad stuff. And expensive. But Pickle was an electrician and always had plenty of money. Maclean remembered Pickle from just after the war as a handsome man, but his hair was going now, and there were long bags under his eyes, and since his wife died a couple of years ago, he seemed sometimes even when you were talking to him to be away somewhere else, like a man with a mortal wound.

"Evenin', Pinky," he said as Maclean sat down. "How ya been?"

Leveret nodded again, this time, in spite of Maclean's beer, more suspicious than magisterial.

"Pretty good," Maclean said.

"I hear you boys had a little dust-up this afternoon," Pickle said.

"Nothing special," Maclean said.

"Jimmy told me," Leveret said, "that Willie Campbell's been goin' around utterin' threats."

"Willie Campbell's always uttering threats," Maclean said. "I wouldn't worry about it if I was you."

He wouldn't need to worry, Maclean thought, because Willie would have sense enough to know that if he went after him or Bill Kayton, he would get himself arrested, and Thurcott would throw him in the jug for a month. And Willie wouldn't go after Ginger because Ginger would probably beat the shit out of him again. It would be himself and Jimmy that Willie would be after because nobody would give a shit what happened to them. Not the law anyway.

"A man can be arrested for utterin' threats," Leveret said.

"Is that a fact?" Pickle said.

"In fact," Leveret said, "he might get more time in jail for utterin' threats than if he just walked up and gave somebody a punch."

"Well, well," Pickle said. "I never understood the law."

So Leveret went on to tell him.

Every once in a while, he would turn to Maclean and ask, "Ain't that so?" and Maclean would say, "That's right, all right."

Otherwise he sipped his beer and calculated. He didn't know Pickle hardly at all compared to Leveret, but Pickle was a good-hearted soul with more money than Leveret ever thought of, and Maclean began to think that by himself, away from Leveret where he wouldn't have to worry about being thought a soft touch, he would be good for half a dollar. He started willing Leveret to get up and go to the can, but he had a bladder like a Saharan camel, and when he had set Pickle straight about the law, he went on to tell him about the war.

"The reason them there Germans invaded Russia," he told Pickle, "is that three or four hundred years ago, the Russians—they was called the moguls in them days—invaded Germany on horseback and burned their houses all down and run off with their women, and the Germans never forgot."

"Is that a fact?" Pickle said.

Since Leveret still showed no signs of moving off and giving him a chance alone with Pickle, Maclean realized that time was running out before the stores closed. He had wasted his money on a god-damned beer he didn't want, and he decided he was just going to have to take whatever chance there was with the two of them together. So edging his way into it as best he could, keeping his voice up just enough to make its way across the table through the uproar, he told them his story about working at Jim Gartley's to get the money for his mother's present and taking it home and hiding it and coming back after they had been at the Black Rock to find it stolen.

Leveret and Pickle both listened with interest at first. Then they began looking down at the table and up at the ceiling and around the room, and Maclean could see that they didn't believe a god-damned word he was saying. They were thinking that even if he had worked at Jim Gartley's stable and earned the money, what had happened was that he had drunk it up.

When he had finished, neither of them even asked him who he thought might have stolen it.

"Well, now," Leveret said, "that is a bad fix."

Maclean had hoped that he wouldn't have to ask outright at all—that just the story would be enough for Pickle anyway to say, "Now look here, I'll lend you a little until your cheque comes in." And if Leveret hadn't been there, Maclean was sure that Pickle would have gone ahead and given him something, if only a quarter. Maclean was so mad at Leveret that he could hardly sit in the chair. Now, even if he did go ahead and ask, he could see that he wasn't going to get anything, not even from Pickle.

"You ain't got no assets you could get some money on?" Leveret asked. "You used to have that there watch. That there watch you brought back from the war. You still got that? You ain't lost it or sold it or nothin'."

"No," Maclean said. "I ain't done anything with it. But I don't think I want to sell that."

"I wasn't thinkin' about that," Leveret said. "I was thinkin' maybe you might get a loan on it. Joe Meltzer sometimes loans a little money on stuff like that."

Maclean had carried that watch for over twenty-five years, one of the few things he had kept through everything. At Festubert, he had taken it out to look at before they went over. He was sure that morning that he was going to be killed, and when he wasn't even scratched, he started to think of it as a good-luck piece. He always looked at it when they were going into danger, and he used to sit holding it when they were being shelled.

"No," Maclean said, "I don't think I want to part with that."

"Let's have a look at it anyway," Leveret said, expansive now that he was sure he wasn't going to be touched for a loan.

Maclean took it out. It was on a leather string tied to a belt loop. He untied it and laid it on the table. It was heavy, silver-coloured, with a white enamel face and elegant Roman numerals for the hours.

"You got it in the war," Leveret said.

"Yes," Maclean said. "I bought it from Bill Perry just before he got killed. He got it off a dead German."

"That looks as if it might be real silver," Pickle said. "It might be worth a lot of money."

"It ain't for sale," Maclean said.

"You could borrow on it just the same," Leveret said.

"It ain't for rent either," Maclean said.

"Let me just have a close look at it," Leveret said, and he picked it up and hefted it.

"That ain't silver," Leveret said. "It ain't really heavy enough for silver, and it ain't the right colour. I seen a lot of silver, and silver is shinier than this. It must be some kind of heavy tin. Ain't that what it is?"

He looked at Pickle.

Pickle looked doubtful, but he was someone who never contradicted people no matter what stupidity he was told.

"Well, maybe," he said.

Leveret turned the watch over and over in his hand, studying it with his best judicial air, and Maclean could see what was coming, which was that Leveret was getting ready to loan him fifty cents on it with the idea that he would never save the fifty cents to get it back. Or if he did, Leveret would have sold it by that time for twenty times the fifty cents.

"It ain't silver," Leveret said. "Anybody who knows can see that, but it's a well-made watch. You'd pay three dollars for a watch like that."

"Well," Maclean said, "if you can buy a watch like that new for three dollars maybe you better go ahead and do it."

"No," Leveret said, "I got a good watch, and I don't really need another, but since you're a little short, I tell you what. I'll buy it off ya for a dollar seein' it's second hand."

"It ain't for sale," Maclean said, " and especially it ain't for sale for any god-damned dollar."

"Now, now," Pickle said.

"Well, then," Leveret said, as if he hadn't heard the last part of what Maclean had said, "suppose I lend you a quarter, and you can give me the watch as cold lateral."

"You cheap, chicken-brained son of a whore," Maclean said, "if you was any kind of friend, you'd lend me a quarter or fifty cents without any watch. It is silver, and you don't know your ass from a hole in the ground, and you never have. Give me my god-damned watch. It ain't for sale, and it ain't for rent."

And he swept the watch up off the table and pushed his chair back so hard he nearly knocked it over, and everyone stopped talking and looked around to see what all the commotion was about.

He stood on the sidewalk at the foot of the steps and considered what to do. It was almost dark now and beginning to get autumnal cool. He should have asked Pickle right out. Even with Leveret there, he would probably have given him at least a quarter. But it was done now, and there was no way he could go back in there. He shouldn't have lost his temper. Losing his temper was something, like a pint of rum, he could only afford the first of the month when his cheque came in.

Down the street, the lights from the Salvation Army chapel fell across the sidewalk. Their service would be over by now, and they would be serving tea and sandwiches and doughnuts to the faithful and anyone else who came to their door. They were good people and good to the soldiers in the war. And if they fussed a little over your soul now and then, they didn't mean any harm, and they'd never tried to make anyone who wasn't an officer feel like dirt the way the Red Cross did.

Maclean walked down the street through the bands of light lying across the sidewalk and stopped by the corner of the chapel. Miss Audrey would be in there. She would have gone to the concert on Main Street, then followed the band back here for the service and talk and sandwiches afterward, putting off the time when she would have to go back to Drusilla's and believing maybe for a little while that there was going to be something more than this up there afterwards. A second chance. But nobody really believed that. They only imagined they did, now and then, for a little while if they didn't think about it too hard. That was why they got up in the middle of the night and knelt by the side of the bed and wept and prayed to the god who wasn't there that before they were struck down they might have a little something of some kind to make them glad they'd been born.

"Did you know," Henry said, "that there's a flower in the Amazon jungle that sits up in a tree and don't have no roots in the ground at all and just lives on air?"

He wondered about going in and asking Miss Audrey for a little loan. She would give it to him. No doubt about it. And not just fifty cents but five dollars if he asked for it and never come after him to pay her back no matter how long it took. That had no doubt been her problem all her life. A little kindness at any price. But if he borrowed from her, he would create a debt that would involve more than money, and he didn't want to do that.

So who? He thought about Henry McDade. One of Drusilla's rules, like not gambling or drinking, was not borrowing money. ("I just don't want no bad feelin's around here," she said. And Elmer said, "Neither a borrower nor a lender be, that's what it says in the Bible.") But Drusilla and Elmer aside, the idea of borrowing money from Henry just didn't feel right. Even if he paid him back the next afternoon, it would change the way Henry thought about him. There was something restful about Henry, like the sound of music somewhere off in the distance, and he didn't want to put that at any kind of risk because of a short-term problem.

He took out his watch and looked at it.

Twenty after nine.

It was going to have to be the watch. At this time of night, he just didn't have any other choice. But he didn't have to sell it. He would borrow on it from Joe Meltzer, and when he got his cheque the end of the month, he would get it back. Everything was going to turn out all right.

11

Maclean tramped back again to the square. The crowds were thinning out now, and lines of cars and trucks with their headlights on were crawling up and down the hill on their way out of town. Maclean imagined them as they might appear to some high-flying nightbird. Tiny swatches of light fanning out across the darkened countryside, along winding country roads, down deep, little valleys, through the black mass of the forest. And behind them, the lights of the town strung out along the river with the brighter band of light that was Main Street running down the middle to this square, where he was picking his way through the traffic, an angular scarecrow in a cloth cap and somebody else's old suitcoat, and somebody else's old trousers, and a pair of somebody else's old boots that weren't going to last him through the winter.

A mud-coloured mongrel tied to the slats on the back of an old half-ton truck bared its teeth and growled at him as he passed. Maclean spat at it out of the side of his mouth, and the dog started to bark. At the top of the square, a loudspeaker outside a music store began playing "Deep in the Heart of Texas."

As he walked up Main Street, he thought hard about the

watch. He recalled what Pickle had said about its being silver and how keen Leveret had suddenly been to get hold of it, and he decided to take it to MacClewan's jewelry store and find out what it was really worth, so he wouldn't end up being cheated this day as well as robbed.

At the corner where the Salvation Army band had been playing, a fat policeman was directing traffic. He gave Maclean a long, hard look, as if wondering if he couldn't think of something to arrest him for. Maclean pretended he didn't see him and concentrated on walking straight and steady.

He stopped in front of the jewelry store and looked into the brightly-lit front shop with its showcases full of rings and necklaces and watches and its wallful of clocks with wagging pendulums all telling him it was twenty-five to ten. At the counter, Mr. Marathon MacClewan was talking earnestly to a large, gray-haired woman in a coat with a collar of red-fox fur complete with the head and glass eyes. As the woman moved, the fox stared out over her shoulder, now at the wagging clocks, now at the traffic outside, now straight at Maclean.

Marathon MacClewan was a tall, cadaverous man with thick glasses, who looked as if God had really intended him to be an undertaker. He was leaning on the counter now, gesturing rhythmically with one hand as if conducting an orchestra, and as he talked and gestured, he looked past the woman and caught sight of Maclean standing in front of his window. He glared at him suspiciously through the thick glasses, which magnified his eyes and made it seem to Maclean as if the fox staring at him over the woman's shoulder had been joined by a Madagascar monkey.

Maclean turned away.

What the hell was he thinking about anyway, he asked himself. If he took his watch in there, MacClewan would think he had stolen it and call the police the minute he was out of the store, and they would throw him in the jug just on the off-chance. What god-damned difference did it make what the watch was worth if he was just going to pawn it? He was wasting time, and if he didn't get a move on, he was going to find Joe Meltzer closed. Leveret would have cheated him. Leveret would cheat his own mother. But Joe Meltzer wasn't going to cheat him. Joe Meltzer was an honest man. That was why he lived upstairs over his store instead of in a big house.

The store was still alight, and in the middle of the great clutter of furniture and lamps and dishes and brasswork and all, Joe was seated at a battered, old dining-room table reading a newspaper. A little bell over the door announced Maclean's entrance, and Joe got up and came towards him in his slow, gently-stepping way, like a man walking around perpetually in a house where someone has just died.

"Hello, Pinky," he said. "Can I do something for you?"

"I need a little money," Maclean said, "and I got this here watch."

He came away from Joe Meltzer's with another two dollars in his pocket. He and Joe had looked over the watch front and back, and Joe said he could loan him five dollars on it, but Maclean didn't want that much because he knew he would spend it and never get the five dollars together to pay Joe back. He had started to ask for just one, then changed his mind and got the two.

Now he walked slowly along the aisles of the five-and-ten-cent store. From behind the cash register, a bald-headed little man with teeth like a groundhog watched his every move, obviously convinced that he had come to steal something, clever shop-lifter that he was, arriving just before closing time when he would be the only person in the store.

He looked at a showcase with boxes of candy. Thanks to the war and the submarines, it would all be sweetened with saccharine instead of sugar and would taste like buttered sawdust. Then there was a showcase of the kind of trashy jewelry a teenager might buy if she was poor and stupid. And a case of little doo-dads like ashtrays with pictures on them of Lake Louise and Mounties on horseback. He stopped at a counter piled with sweaters. She always felt the cold, even in summer, the way he himself had begun to do, as the furnace of life began not to burn too well, except when stoked with some rum.

The bald-headed man came over as soon as he stopped.

"Yessss?" he said, his breath whistling through the groundhog teeth.

"I want to buy a sweater for my mother," Maclean told him.

The clerk looked at him as if searching for some devilish plot behind this.

"I ain't sure about the size."

"Mrs. MacPhedran will look after you," the man said.

He gestured grandly to a woman on the other side of the store and went back to his cash register.

"Hello, John," Mrs. MacPhedran said. "What can I do for you?"

Mrs. MacPhedran was the wife of one of the boys from

the war, but her husband was off now in the Veteran's Guard at a prisoner-of-war camp somewhere. Between them, they found a sky-blue sweater that should fit, and Mrs. MacPhedran got a box and wrapped it up in brown paper and decorated it with some ribbons she found lying around in the back shop.

The sweater cost a dollar and twenty-nine cents. This was more than he had spent in a long time, but it still left him with nearly a dollar. He felt the familiar thirst at the back of his throat, but first before any more calamities befell, he would deliver the present. Then the quenching of his thirst would be all the sweeter.

"A joy deferred," Miss Audrey was fond of saying, "is a joy enhanced."

His parcel hanging loose in one hand, Maclean stood in the entrance to the Carleton Hotel, cursing to himself the bad luck, in this day of bad luck, that had brought him there just at that minute. On the sidewalk, not six feet away, Willie Campbell, Junior Tedley, and two of Willie's pals from across the river stood with their backs to him looking up and down Main Street. He had heard them at the very last second coming around the corner and had just managed to get in here out of their way.

He watched them thread their way through the crawling lines of traffic and make the sidewalk on the other side of the street. They were all drunk, Willie especially, weaving one leg over the other, tossing his shoulders around, rolling his head from side to side like a scavenging bear. Once across the street, they stopped again at the entrance to an alley, evidently trying to decide where to go next. Finally, after a lot of talking and waving around of arms, while they leaned on each other and shuffled back and forth to keep their feet underneath them, they set off into the alley, and Maclean began to think that he was out of it without any more trouble—not that Willie was in a shape to cause much trouble to anybody.

Then, as if the chicken-brained son of a whore had eyes in the back of his head, Junior turned around and looked straight at him. He peered as if making sure he was seeing what he was seeing, then shouted for Willie. Willie got himself turned around, and Junior pointed, his whole arm outstretched like a lookout in a movie who has spotted land or a whale.

Willie looked along the outstretched arm and got Maclean into focus.

"Pinky, you bastard!" he bellowed. "You son of a whore, you pull a knife on me,"

He stormed back out of the alley, waving his fists like a madman. His other two pals took in what was happening and went blundering after him. They caught up with him at the edge of the sidewalk. Groping around, like men in a pitch-dark cellar, they managed to fasten onto him, one to an arm, one to the back of his collar and got him stopped. While he roared and shook himself half out of his coat, they shouted into his ears and pointed down the hill at the fat policeman in the middle of the street directing traffic.

They scuffled back and forth, scattering pedestrians and looking every second as if they were all going to fall down in a heap. Then Willie got loose and staggered out between two parked cars. His face was as dirty as if he'd been working all day in a ditch, and Maclean could see the thick foam of spittle at the corners of his mouth.

"Pinky, you bastard," he shouted through the traffic. "I'll get you, you pig-fucking son of a whore. I'll get you."

His two pals squeezed between the cars and got hold of him again, and Willie wrestled and swore. But Maclean could see that it was now all just show, so that afterwards he could tell anybody who would listen that if it hadn't been that the boys held him back, by Jesus, he would have gone across that god-damned street, and to hell with the god-damned cars and to hell with the god-damned policeman, and he would have beaten that bastard Maclean, by Jesus, right there in front of the whole town, and he wouldn't have given a shit if they'd put him in jail for a year for it because that, by Jesus, was the kind of man he was.

After one last scuffle, arms and legs flying everywhere, he let himself be herded off, half-walking, half dragged along, roaring and cursing, into the alley.

"Pinky, you yellow-bellied bastard. You pull a knife on me. You rotten piece of dog-shit..."

Maclean stopped by the ruins of the stone gate-posts at the foot of the drive. He had walked fast the whole half-mile uphill from downtown, and he was breathing hard, his heart pounding heavily as if it were being slapped back and forth like a roll of bread dough. There was a pain under his breast-bone. (It isn't just the lungs, Mr. Maclean. These things put a strain on the heart too, so don't overexert yourself. Avoid excitement.) He coughed hard and started to take out the five-pack of Turrets he had bought at a filling station at the foot of the hill. But they wouldn't let him smoke inside, and he didn't want to ruin a good tailor-made by stubbing it out and lighting it up again, and he didn't want to take the time to smoke it out here. That too could wait, then both together, a cigarette and a glass of rum, in a snug, warm refuge he already had in mind, safe for a while from everything inside and out.

He turned up the drive. The house stood back from the street in the centre of a sloping lawn bordered by a line of old oak and maple trees. The house was old too, as old almost as the trees, and large and grand with stone front steps and bay windows upstairs and down. It had been built by a family that once had lots of money, but they had lost it all somehow sometime after Confederation, and then they had all died or got killed in the war or moved away, and the house was sold to someone, who sold it to someone else, who sold it at last to a woman who made it over into a "Home"—which is to say, one of Dr. Death's waiting-rooms.

Maclean climbed the stone steps, pushed open the heavy door, and stepped inside into the sour smell of sickness and age. There was no one around, and only two lights with low-watt bulbs were burning in little brass brackets on the wall. To the right, a staircase with ornamental oak banisters ran up to a higher zone of twilight, where those still able to climb stairs did their waiting. To the left, a corridor ran off towards the back of the house, lined with doors like the corridor of a hotel, where the dining room and parlours of the old house had been cut up to make rooms for the 'guests.'

Half way along the corridor, a shrunken, little old man was pushing a four-legged, wooden walker ahead of him. Maclean recognized him behind this hideous disguise as a man, once very brisk and dapper, who had worked in a bank. Brisk and dapper no more, he would push the walker an inch or two ahead, then with immense effort push first one foot, then the other, after it, his eyes fixed fiercely ahead of him, like the eyes of a soldier, dying and demented, crawling back through the mud to the trench he had just climbed out of.

Unnoticed, Maclean sidled past him and found the door of his mother's room open. She was sitting in her rocking chair in a padded dressing gown, her back half-turned to him, her eyes closed. Her hair was so thinned he could see the shape of her skull through it. Her face was white, her cheek bony, her hand on the arm of the chair skeletal.

He walked around the chair, and she started and opened her eyes. Behind her glasses, they had a strange, transparent look. Dark brown once and large, the brown now looked as if it had faded, like old cloth in the sun.

"John, I didn't hear you come in. Have you been here long?"

"No, Mamma. Just now. Just this minute. I came up to bring you your birthday present."

He held out the box.

"Oh, John, you shouldn't spend your money on presents."

"It isn't anything expensive."

She hefted it in her hand, then passed it back to him.

"Not heavy. Must be something nice. Why don't you put it over on the table by the window. I'll open it in the morning. My grandfather used to say that it meant bad luck for the whole year if you opened your birthday present before your birthday."

He put the parcel down on the table in front of a cluster of old photographs like the ones he had seen at Alice's and drew a chair over beside his mother and sat down.

"It's been a long time since you were here," she said. "How have you been keeping?"

"Good. Fine."

"You still haven't found another job?"

"No, Mamma. Not yet. But I still have my pension."

"You're not going hungry?"

"No, no. Nothing like that."

"And you got a good place to live?"

"Yes, yes."

"And you still got your health, that's a great thing."

"Yes. Perfect. No problems."

"Well, that's good. I worry about you. You should have found someone and got married after the war. It would have been better. You used to go with that girl in town for a while when you were in school. I don't remember her name."

"Cynthia."

"That's right. She got married."

"Yes, she got married."

"I saw her going by on the street one day when I was sitting out front."

"She moved away, Mamma. She moved away over twenty years ago. You must have seen someone else."

"No, I always notice the way she walks."

"Mamma, she's nearly fifty years old now."

"Well, it doesn't matter."

"Anyway," she added, "I'm glad you stopped seeing that Swann woman. I'm glad she went away. She wasn't the right sort of person."

She began to rock, as if all of a sudden, she had lost interest in the conversation or forgotten he was there.

He remembered only now that he was here that it was always like this. He sat for a few minutes, then got up and walked over to the window.

Outside, he could see the shadowy forms of the trees, the ruins of a picket fence, a gazebo with mouldering shingles, all silvery in the moonlight. And a reflection of himself looking back at him so faint, so indistinct, that it might have been the ghost of a younger self come through the desolation of the garden to stare at what he had become. Beyond the reflection of himself, he became aware of two points of light like glowing embers, and around them a raccoon took shape among the trees. It paused, then half-stood, heaved itself around, and vanished back into the shadows.

"I remember this house when I was a little girl," his mother said suddenly. "A family named Burnside lived here, and they had two girls who were just a little bit older than I was, and I came here once for a birthday party out there in the yard, and there was a terrible thunder storm, and we all had to run inside. Isn't it funny that I'm living here after all these years. What would they think if they could see it now? I wonder what ever happened to them. You never heard?"

"No, Mamma, I never knew them."

A fat girl in a ratty, flowered dress, hanging crooked at the hem, appeared at the door. She was smiling. The smile faltered as she caught sight of him, then, between one footstep and the next, recovered itself, and she came bustling in.

"I just come in to make sures there ain't nothin' you wanted before you went to bed, Mrs. Maclean," she said.

Mrs. Maclean turned in her chair.

"This is my son John," she said.

"Hi," the girl said. "Ain't that nice you come to see your mother. She's been pretty good lately, ain't you, Mrs. Maclean. Yes, we have, ain't we?"

"Not too bad," Mrs. Maclean said.

The girl went bustling about the room, straightening up the towels on the rack, moving the pictures on the table half an inch this way, half an inch that, peeking into the wastebasket, and prattling all the time in an itty-bitty voice like someone talking to a small child or an imbecile.

"This is Katey," Mrs. Maclean said.

The girl went over to the bed, and Maclean moved out of her way back against the window. She unfolded a wool blanket from the foot of the bed and spread it out and turned down the sheets, the tops of her big breasts bulging out over the V-neck of her dress. One of those sloppy, well-upholstered girls who seem to have a hard time staying inside their clothes. Like Elsie Skadgett.

Elsie was dead now almost twenty-five years. Nothing left of her in the ruins of her cheap coffin but a few bones. It didn't take long. A shell would send the bones from last year's battle flying. Except that sometimes the dead got buried deeper, down in the mud where there wasn't any air, and what came up then was something else. Like green bread dough. A stink like nothing else in the world. Terrifying. Worse than shells. Worse than mortars.

Maclean turned away and looked out the window again. The moon had come up over the roof of the house and was shining on the tops of the trees. Below them, the shadows moved, and Maclean saw that the big raccoon had been joined by three kits, who were snuffling busily around in the grass and dead leaves. Somewhere in the distance, a dog barked, and they all lifted their sharp faces and listened.

"And tomorrow's your birthday," the girl was saying. "Ain't that nice."

"John brought me a present," Mrs. Maclean said. "There

on the table. But I don't open it until tomorrow because it would be bad luck."

"You can open it when you get to your daughter's maybe," the girl said. "And we'll get some nice presents there, I'll bet, now won't we?"

So that's what all the cooking had been about at Alice's, Maclean realized. She would have them all in—her daughters and their husbands and kids. And it would all be in the local paper.

He looked at the reflection of his mother sitting in her chair, fainter even than his own reflection, but he could see that she was watching him furtively, guiltily, unaware that he was watching her back.

"I expect you'll be at the party too, Mr. Maclean," the girl was saying to him.

"No," Maclean said, not turning away from the window. "No."

"Oh," the girl said.

"Quite a crowd with all the kids," Maclean said. "A little too much noise for me."

"I suppose," the girl said.

No wonder Alice had been so jumpy when he arrived. He had stumbled in on her preparations, and she was worried he would guess. He wondered if they had thought of asking him. Probably not. He had passed out of their world a long time ago, and they didn't want to think about him. And he couldn't blame them too much for that. Still. All that fuss about the present. Working. Getting robbed. Nearly getting killed on the god-damned railroad bridge. Why? For what? Perhaps the same insane notion that had taken him to Alice's that afternoon, the notion that took shape somewhere out of the reach of reason, the notion that somehow at Alice's or here some miraculous act of transportation would take him back into the past so that everything that had gone bad could be made to happen in a different way. Crazy. Or perhaps it was just that he was one of those fools who couldn't leave their wounds alone but had to keep worrying them until they started to bleed again.

(It isn't the soul that goes on making you the same person, Henry, it's memory, the cells passing it down from one generation to the next like an hereditary disease.)

Outside, the raccoons had come out of the trees onto the lawn and were making their way towards the back of the house, towards the garbage cans maybe or a stand of corn. They moved cautiously, the mother in front, the three kits trotting behind her in a row.

His father used to have a dog—a nasty, little, black mongrel that no one could go near but himself. He used it to hunt down rats and anything else than strayed onto his property. Once they cornered a female raccoon and two kits in a corner of the back field. The mother could have gotten away through the fence if she had abandoned the kits because the mongrel would have been no match for her if he had caught up with her in the woods. But she stayed, backed up against the fence with the kits behind her. His father shot her first, then the two kits, and left the bodies there as a warning to anything else that dared invade the sacred territory of Angus Maclean.

The girl was still chattering away to his mother about the birthday party, and his mother was still watching him as she half-listened.

She could have stood up for him, but she never did. She

abandoned him. And Alice. They could have gone on through school. They could have had another life. She was too weak, too scared of that wretched excuse for a human being whom she must once have mistaken for a figure of manly strength. She never saw that he was a coward as well as a bully—not a fearsome instrument of God, just a squalid, mean little devil. Why didn't she leave him? Why didn't she take Alice and him and go back across the river to her own people? They would have looked after us. They would have seen to it that we all had a good life. As it was, all she had done was to allow him enough education to make him feel too good for the likes of Elsie or Claudine and not good enough for the likes of Cynthia. Well, to hell with it.

He turned towards her. For a moment she studied him with the same furtive look he had seen reflected in the window, but he had made his face a blank. All he wanted now was to be out of here.

The girl had left off her chatter and was counting out pills from some little bottles on the dresser.

"I guess it must be getting to be your bedtime," he said. "I better be on my way."

"Yes," she said. "I'm beginning to feel a little tired."

"That's right," the girl said. "We need our rest, don't we? And we got a big day tomorrow."

She brought the pills and a glass of water, and his mother swallowed them one by one with a sip of water between, dutifully, pathetically, like a child. What did she think about here in her long nights alone? Did she too sometimes think about those forks in the road she hadn't taken? Did she ever dream about those days in her father's house among the sinners bound for eternal damnation that Mr. Angus Maclean had rescued her from and taken such care that his children should not be corrupted by? Perhaps out of reach of everybody and everything, that was where she now lived, quietly, unobtrusively, not letting anyone know that she had moved, this room, this dreadful place, a mere shadow, and he himself a mere shadow too.

"You've got a long walk home," she said when she had swallowed the last of the pills. "Clear to Chapel Street."

"No, Mamma," he said. "I moved from Chapel Street a long time ago. I live down on the flat now."

"Oh, yes," she said. "I remember."

"Good night then," she said.

"And thank you for the present," the girl prompted.

"Oh, yes," she said. "And thank you for the present. It was good of you to remember."

12

As he walked on towards the edge of town, Maclean looked up at the sky, high and hard, with an almost full moon and thousands of stars, and upriver, faint, shimmering waves of northern lights, like the flickering of a distant barrage, too far away to be heard, off towards the Chemin des Dames, where the French would be dying. Adieu la vie. Adieu l'amour. Le jour du gloire est arrivé.

Miss Mazerolle pounds the old high school piano and sings. Allons, enfants de la Patrie. She can't play worth a shit, and she has a voice like wind in the stovepipes, but she loves France. She had been there once, thirty years before, for a month and had spent the rest of her life talking about it, showing people her yellowing photographs, giving little lectures in the basement of the library. When he got back, she met him one day on the street. Getting old, graying, frail, her shoulders humped, her body twisted with arthritis.

"Did you see Paris?" she asked him. "Did you see Paris?"

"No, I never got the chance."

"What a pity! All my life I remembered Paris. It was spring. Such a beautiful city."

The little packed-mud and gravel road Maclean's feet at last carried him to angled off across the face of the hill, its uphill side bordered by a forest of black fir trees, the down-hill side cleared, falling away towards the moonlit river far below. There were houses scattered along both sides of the road. The biggest were plain, square, two-storey frames, the smallest, hardly more than shacks. The electric light came only to the first houses on the road, where wires had been hauled across from a more prosperous street nearby. The rest were lighted with kerosene lamps, their windows mellow-orange and soft in the darkness the way windows used to be everywhere when he was a child.

Ellie Deboys' house was one of the last on the uphill side of the road, standing back in a little, square clearing in the fir trees, a story-and-a-half cottage with a string of additions trailing off the back—a kitchen, some sheds, an outhouse.

The lamps were lit in the kitchen and the curtains drawn.

As Maclean approached the kitchen door, he heard a murmur of voices. Except for Ellie's, he couldn't make out whose, and he paused to listen. A big, shambling dog, like a fat sheep, came out of the shed and said "gwuff," then put its front paws out along the ground and stretched itself. This was Dreadnought, whose job was to raise the alarm at the approach of strangers, but Maclean was no stranger, and Dreadnought's sagacious senses never mistook. Inside, however, his greeting had been heard, and the voices faltered their way into silence.

On the window sill beside the kitchen door, four tin cans of geraniums stood in a row, two small cans, a larger can, another small can. Maclean studied them, then knocked carefully. Knock. Knock. Knock, knock. Knock. The door in front of Maclean was divided two thirds of the way up like the door of a stable. The top part opened cautiously half way, and Ellie's head and shoulders appeared. The bottom part remained closed and bolted. This was another of Ellie's careful protections of herself, like the tin cans with stones in them hung on strings wound through the trees at the edge of the yard to alert Dreadnought to the approach of snoopers or thieves or rapists or the police.

Ellie was a big woman, her shoulders and neck softly massive. Her hair was thick and gray, her skin the colour of milk chocolate. She peered out at Maclean.

"Well, now, Mr. John Maclean," she said. "I ain't seen you for a long time. I'm surprised Dreadnought ain't gone and forgot you."

"Dogs never forget," Maclean said.

"I guess not," she said. "Dogs and Irishmen."

She unbolted the bottom of the door, and Maclean stepped inside, into the warmth and lamplight and the smell of baking bread. Along with her other wares, Ellie sold bread and rolls.

On the end wall of the kitchen, where the chimney of the original house still stood, indoors now instead of out, a black woodstove was blazing away cooking the bread. At the other end of the kitchen, two men were sitting at a big dropleaf table, their hands clasped in front of them as if they were engaged in an act of religious meditation. From behind some pickle jars on a cupboard shelf, Ellie took two half-filled glasses and put them down in front of them. The only other thing on the table was a single ashtray with a single cigarette burning in it and looking somehow disowned as if the person smoking it had just disappeared out the window.

If there was anyone in town over the age of five who didn't know that Ellie bootlegged, it could only have been someone who had just got off a train, but nobody had ever done anything about it, and it didn't seem likely that anyone ever would. Ellie probably knew that, but it gave her a sense of importance to think that she was defying the law and that some night carloads of Mounties in red coats might come screaming up to her door. Ellie was a religious woman, but religion was one thing and the law was another, and there was nowhere in the Ten Commandments nor anywhere else in the Bible that she had ever heard of where it was forbidden that a man have a drink in moderation and in good humour among his friends, just the way the Lord himself had done.

"Evening, Johnny," Maclean said. "Evening, Ralph."

Johnny Doone was a little Irishman from a village out in the woods that had been settled by Catholic Irish so much to the exclusion of anybody else that the people there still had their accents after a hundred years. He worked at the railway yard and made good money but for some reason had never married.

Ralph Gowrie was an old veteran, a carpenter, who also made good money and had married but whose wife had dropped dead several years before while watching a horse race. He lived only a quarter of a mile from Ellie's on the street with the electricity. He had been walking by one day and saw a loose clapboard on Ellie's house and went home and got a hammer and nailed it back on and had got in the habit on a Saturday night of dropping in for a little tot of rum before going home to his solitary bed.

Maclean sat down at the table and got a pony of Black

Diamond Demerara and a glass. He poured a little into his glass, put the bottle away in his coat pocket, and settled back into his chair, letting the warmth of the room begin to fold him into itself.

"We was taaalkin'," Johnny said, broadening the "a" out in the back of his throat, "about bears."

"We was talkin'," Ralph said, "about the time that bear come out of the woods here and Dreadnought was gonna fight it."

It was a story that had been told a hundred times over the years, gathering around itself an atmosphere of tranquil predictability like that of a bedtime story.

One fall, Ellie heard a commotion outside, first the clatter, by the sound of it, of every can she had hung up in the trees, then the sound of Dreadnought, a young dog then, howling and growling the way he could have wakened the dead. When Ellie went out, there at the edge of the woods was the biggest bear she had ever seen, and in front of the bear all ready to fight it was Dreadnought. The bear swung at Dreadnought, and Dreadnought jumped out of the way, but he wasn't going to run. He was going to stay there and fight and get himself killed. So Ellie went into the kitchen and got a little washtub and a stick of hardwood and came storming out, beating the bottom of the tub for all she was worth. The bear took one look and ran. On its way, it got tangled up in more of the strings with the tin cans full of stones, and you could still hear it a quarter of a mile away tearing off through the woods with the tin cans jangling along behind it.

"Dreadnaaaught," Johnny repeated, "is a great dog."

Their contemplation of the heroics of Dreadnought was broken into by a complicated ratty-tat-tat-tiddly-tat-tat-tiddly-tat-tat-tat on the top part of the outside door. Ellie went over and leaned her ear against it.

"Is that you, Legs?" she asked.

"No," a put-on raspy voice said through the door, "it's the sheriff and the chief of police and two mounties and the head of the boy scouts and three fierce ladies from the WCTU with billy clubs and axes, and we all come to put you wicked people in there in jail."

Ellie unbolted both halves of the door, and a tall, lean, laughing old man with a long lantern-jawed face and a bald head stepped into the room, one long leg with elaborate slowness after the other.

"Some day, you come here and do that, and I'm gonna set Dreadnought on you," Ellie said.

"Dreadnought wouldn't bite me," Legs said. "Truth is, I don't think he'd bite nobody. You might as well have a pet pussy cat out there."

"Ain't so," Ellie said.

"Remember the bear," Johnny said.

"What bear?" Legs said. "I ain't heard nothin' about no bear. You ain't gonna tell me some big lie about old Dreadnought standin' up to some bear."

Legs was a cousin of Ellie's at a different generational level. His real name was Joshua Deboys, and some of the family called him Josh, but everyone else called him Legs because at one time, long ago around the turn of the century, he had been a step-dancer. Mostly he just danced around town for the fun of it, but he had once danced at some kind of vaudeville show in Fredericton for money and got mentioned in the paper.

"Legs," Ellie said, "don't you ever talk any kind of sense?

You tease me hard enough and you're gonna get a swipe of this across the side of the head."

She picked the rolling pin up off the cupboard and waved it at him.

Legs put his hands up over his head.

"You want some buttermilk or what?" Ellie asked.

"Yes, thank you," Legs said. "That'd be good."

Ellie went out to the shed where she kept her ice box and came back with a gallon wine jug half full of buttermilk. Legs fetched a glass down out of the cupboard, and Ellie carefully poured it.

"Two cents," Ellie said.

"Suppose I split you some wood come Monday, how'd that be?"

"O.K.," Ellie said. "But don't you forget, or you won't see no more buttermilk or nothin' else around here."

Legs sipped the buttermilk and licked his upper lip.

"You hear about the McIntyre boy?" Ellie asked when she had put away the buttermilk.

"Yes," Legs said. "I been over."

"I ain't been," Ellie said. "I'll maybe go over tomorrow."

"You all heard about the McIntyre boy got killed in the army?" Legs asked the others. "Him that used to box?"

"Yes," they said.

"Sam is takin' it bad," Legs said. "Even worse than Amanda."

"It's a terrible thing," Ralph said, "to lose a son."

"I think old Sam would a hundred times more sooner of died himself," Legs said.

"What did he want to go over there for anyways," Ellie said. "He didn't have to go. They hadn't called him up or nothin'. And even if they had, he didn't need to go over there. He could of just set around like them soldiers downtown."

"I guess he wasn't that kind of boy," Ralph said. "We was the same, John, wasn't we?"

"I guess so," Maclean said.

"So tell me why," Ellie said. "Just tell me what kind of sense there is to it."

"There ain't no sense to it," Ralph said. "But when you're young, you're stupid. You want to be a hero and all that kind of stuff."

"And you want to get away and be your own man for a change," Maclean said.

Ellie snorted.

"The only people wars do any good to," she said, "are the rich people. You don't see them over there gettin' themselves killed. They're all back here rakin' in the money."

"True," Maclean said.

"But there was good times too," Ralph said. "Some of the best times of our lives, wasn't they? We were young, and we had wonderful pals would do anything for you. Like brothers. Better maybe than brothers. I sometimes think there ain't never been anything like that since."

"That's true too," Maclean said.

"Good times," Ellie said, "unless you get killed like the McIntyre boy."

There was a silence, and they all sat around looking down at their glasses and thinking about the McIntyre boy.

"Now, what would you do," Johnny asked, changing the subject after a respectful minute or two, "if you had a million dollars?"

"Well," Ralph said, settling back in his chair and thinking about it, "a man don't need no million dollars, but ten thousand would go down pretty good."

"Twenty," Johnny said. "Let's make it twenty. Somewhere in the world, you could have a long-lost relative could die and leave you twenty."

The talk drifted away into sunlit pastures of fantasy. Buying of houses and farms. Buying of horses and cars. Journeys to south sea islands of perpetual summer.

Outside the door, Dreadnought stirred and made vague mouthing sounds as if he were chewing a bone. Ralph and Johnny leaped to hide their glasses in the cupboard, and Maclean put his on his lap under the leaf of the table.

There was a pause, then the coded knock on the door.

Ellie unbolted the top part of the door and opened it a few inches, and the light fell on a long simpleton's face topped with a swatch of brick-red hair that stuck out in all directions like the hair of a cartoon character who has just stuck his finger into a light socket.

It was Waldo Dumbar, a gangling young man who lived a couple of miles up the road and sometimes stopped in at Ellie's on a Saturday night on his way home from his job in a store downtown.

"You still up?" he asked Ellie.

"No," Ellie said, "I'm upstairs asleep."

She opened the rest of the door, and he stepped inside.

He settled himself at the table, and Ellie poured him a cup of tea. Ellie never allowed Waldo alcohol because after a drink or two he became a crazy man running up and down the road shouting and falling into the ditch and wanting to fight with everybody he met.

While Ralph and Johnny had been dreaming about

money, Ellie had taken the bread out of the oven, half a dozen loaves, butter-gold on top. She sliced a loaf now and put half a dozen slices in the middle of the table.

"That'll be two cents," she said to Waldo, "and I don't need no wood split."

Maclean would have liked the heel of the loaf, but Waldo got to it first and slathered it with butter and stuffed it into his face and licked around his lips like a dog.

"Bad accident downtown tonight," he said.

Nobody ever paid any attention to Waldo because he never said anything worth paying attention to. Legs and Ellie started talking again about the McIntyre boy. Johnny and Ralph got into talk about jobs on the railroad. Maclean let his mind drift away into a warm nothingness.

"Kilt him right there," Waldo was saying, talking away to himself. "Kilt him right there on the bridge."

"Kilt who?" Ellie asked him finally.

"That there man on the bridge," Waldo said. "I been tryin' to tell ya. That there man on the bridge got run over and kilt."

"What there man, Waldo?" Ralph asked.

"Willie Campbell," Waldo said. "You all know Willie Campbell."

"Who?" Maclean asked.

"Willie Campbell," Waldo said. "He was walkin' across the bridge goin' home, and he was walkin' with his back to the traffic, and somehow he seems to just have stepped out away from the rail in front of a truck, and it knocked him down and run right over him before the man drivin' it had a chance to do a thing. Kilt him dead right there."

"Did you see it?" Johnny asked.

"No," Waldo said, "I never seen it. But some men come into the store that seen it and told us all about it, so it's the truth, and there ain't no doubt."

"Was he drinkin'?" Johnny asked.

"That's what they say," Waldo said. "They say he got into a fight with somebody in front of the Farmer's Store and got knocked down and his face all bloodied up, and they say later on he was so drunk he couldn't hardly stand up and all covered with dirt and blood down the front of his shirt."

"Are you sure it was Willie Campbell?" Maclean asked.

"Yes," Waldo said. "Everybody said. And some of them was out there and seen."

"And it killed him?"

"Yes," Waldo said. "It kilt him dead right there. A great, big wood truck, and it run right over him. They say it squooshed his chest right out flat. And his eyes and his tongue...."

"All right, Waldo," Ellie said, "we don't need no pictures."

"Well, well," Ralph said. "Now ain't that somethin'?"

"No great loss to the world," Johnny said.

"All the same," Legs said.

Maclean looked down at his glass of rum and his cigarette burning in the ashtray. He couldn't even pretend to himself that he was sorry for Willie Campbell. Some day, a week from now or a month or three months, Willie would have caught him alone in an alley with no policeman around, and he was going to end up beaten half to death. Now he was rescued. It was bad luck to feel glad about anybody's death, no matter whose, but he was glad all the same.

"Run right over him," Waldo said, wanting to go on being the centre of attention. "Squooshed him right out flat."

"Shut up, Waldo," Ellie said.

Maclean finished the rum in his glass and excused himself and made his way out through the shed to the outhouse and stood in the darkness.

On his way back to the kitchen, he stopped in the open door of the shed and leaned against the frame and looked out. Dreadnought got himself to his feet and shuffled over. Maclean scratched his ears, and he shook his great sheepskin hide and shuffled back to his spot outside the kitchen door and dropped himself down.

In the woods, the moonlight cast a network of shadows, and there were small sounds. A bird restless in its nest. (Did they dream?) Crickets. Rustling sounds too faint to identify, the movement of small animals going about their business, or maybe just a breath of wind, like a sigh, among the fir boughs. Fall was almost here, then winter. Snow drifted under the trees and piled high against the house beside the shoveled path. The big kitchen stove roaring with hardwood.

He thought again about Willie Campbell. Bad luck or no bad luck, he still couldn't feel sorry. He wouldn't have brought it about if it had been in his power to bring it about. And if it had been in his power to save him, he would have had to save him. But it didn't have anything to do with him. It just happened, and whether he was glad or sorry didn't make any difference.

He remembered the day Akers got killed. Sergeant Death himself. A bolt from the blue. Nobody heard it fired. Nobody heard it coming. It hit just in the angle of the trench. Most of the blast went the other way down the next traverse, but Akers was standing just by the angle. When they got themselves up, there was Akers all covered with dirt and one of his legs blown off above the knee and pouring blood. He clawed around on the ground, his eyes wild, squealing and gurgling like a pig with its throat half cut. Someone tried to get a tourniquet on the leg, but it wasn't any use. Those big arteries went on pumping out blood, and in a couple of minutes more he was dead, his eyes rolling back into his head, and black blood pouring out of his mouth from the burst lungs that would have killed him anyway.

He hadn't wanted to feel glad about that death either, but he had, and so had everybody else. ("Bye, bye, Sergeant Death," someone had said.) There was even a crazy feeling that now that Sergeant Death had been killed, nobody else would get killed any more forever. And for the rest of that turn in the line nobody had.

But, of course, Death hadn't died, and their next turn in, they lost ten men killed without any real fighting at all, just to snipers and random shrapnel.

It wasn't long after that that they took him out for good. One day, carrying a load of lumber up through the communication trench, he collapsed, and when they got him back to the field hospital, he started spitting blood, so they sent him to hospital in England, and after a few weeks, a doctor decided his lungs were damaged, and he should never have been sent back after Ypres at all.

He was going home. He was going to live. He could hardly believe it, and all the way over he was sure they were going to be torpedoed before they got him home. Then early one morning, they saw big, black gulls over the ship and a few hours later the coast of Nova Scotia, a long, low outline on the horizon like a bank of cloud. That evening they docked in Saint John. It was spring, leaves coming out, everything soft and warm. He still couldn't believe it. For days, weeks, he couldn't believe it.

He took the bottle out of his pocket and took a short swig, and went on standing for a while longer before he made his way back through the woodshed to the kitchen.

He sat down again in his place by the table, tipped a little rum into his glass, and added water.

The deaths of the McIntyre boy and Willie Campbell had been talked out, and the conversation had drifted off into the past, as it often did near the end of an evening.

"I seen you dance once," Ralph was saying to Legs. "Way back before the Great War. Down at the Salvation Army at a concert they gave there to raise money for something."

"That's right," Legs said. "Long time ago. Long time. And Ellie here sang in a chorus with a bunch of other girls. What did you sing, Ellie?"

"I don't know," Ellie said. "I don't remember. It was a long time ago, just like you said."

"You sang 'Old Rugged Cross,'" Legs said.

"May be," Ellie said. "I don't remember."

Maclean looked at Ellie and tried to imagine her young. He had never seen her then, not that he remembered anyway, but maybe he had and hadn't known it. Maybe one day he had seen a girl who was Ellie walking down the street or standing outside the Salvation Army. And Ellie had maybe seen him too as a boy that long-ago day.

"There's a man somewhere," Maclean said, "who says that all the time that ever was, and all the things that ever happened, are still here now, only in a different place."

"I don't understand that, John," Ralph said. "You say some funny things sometimes."

"You gonna sing that song for us again, Ellie?" Legs asked.

"No, I ain't."

"You used to play the banjo," Ralph said to Legs. "You don't no more?"

"No, I don't, not no more," Legs said. "I sold that banjo a long time ago. My fingers got too stiff to play it right, and I didn't like playin' it wrong, and it just hung on the wall there lookin' at me, so one day I up and sold it to a man had been wantin' to buy it for a long time. I was sorry afterwards. But I wasn't gonna play it again. Not in this lifetime. Nor dance no more neither."

Outside the window, Dreadnought gwuffed once, then again a little louder, and they all stopped to listen. But they couldn't hear anything and Dreadnought settled down again. Somewhere beyond the reach of their human senses, somewhere out in the woods in the darkness, something had been making its way, looking for something to eat, or trying to keep from being eaten.

The talk drifted on aimlessly, circling for a while around the coming of winter, then drifting away again into hunting and the potato crop and the low water in the river, all these things touched on only, turned this way and that as if all of them sitting there around the table were somehow beyond the consequences attaching to any of these matters, looking down on them from some Olympian height, remote and invulnerable.

Maclean sat, half-listening, letting his eyes roam about the familiar room. The cookstove. The pine cupboards with their neat rows of glasses and dishes. The scrubbed floor.

The white and blue check curtains. The kerosene lamps. The smell of bread, the rambling talk, the warmth. It was good. It was the way the rest of the world should be but, of course, never would.

He thought again of building himself a little house. Somewhere along this road maybe, so that he could drop up here of an evening and sip a little of Ellie's rum and sit in the warmth and have quiet talks with Ralph and Johnnie and Legs. A quarter of an acre of land would do him—space for the house and a garden where he could grow some of his own food. He could lease the land and not have to get together the money to buy it outright. People would lease land without too much fuss because they could always get it back if need be. He wasn't going to eat it up or burn it down or drive it over the bank into the river. And he could do most of the building himself with a little help maybe from Bill Kayton, who always knew where there was lumber lying around that nobody wanted.

A settled man with his own house, small maybe but his own.

The face of Claudine Swann once again began to take shape in his mind.

(Why not? Why in Christ's name not? Go away. Go away, god damn it, and leave me alone. I know why not, and I already know that it shouldn't have happened the way it happened. So go away.)

He looked at his glass and saw that it was empty. He took the bottle out of his pocket and considered the couple of fingers that were left and decided that for the moment he would leave them. It might be nice to have a little tot somewhere on the long walk home.

He settled back in his chair, adding a comment now and then to the conversation, but mostly just listening. Once he reached for his watch and found it gone and took a second to remember, then turned and looked at Ellie's clock on a shelf behind him.

After a while Waldo got up to go. He went out and closed the door behind him and Dreadnought went "gwuff." Then Ralph and Johnny left, and there was only himself and Legs and Ellie. He didn't feel like going, but it was late, and he could see that Ellie was wanting to go to bed. He got up at last, and Legs got up with him.

"I ain't forgot you owe to split me some wood come Monday," Ellie said to Legs.

She let them out and watched over the top half of the door as they walked down the yard.

Except for the lights behind them at Ellie's place, there were no lights now anywhere along the road. Legs lived nearly at the end of the road with his mother. She was almost a hundred years old, though nobody knew for sure, including herself probably, and there were stories that she had been a runaway slave who made it to Canada after all sorts of adventures. Nobody knew anything about that for sure either, and nobody Maclean knew had ever thought it proper to ask Legs.

"Ellie surely keeps a nice place," Legs said when they were stopped in front of his house. "I surely would miss that place if anything ever happened to her. Ain't many pleasures left in the world come our age, now is there?"

"No, there ain't," Maclean said.

"You all right, then?" Legs asked.

"Sure," Maclean said. "I'm just fine. Never better."

"You get home all right? Long way down there."

"I'm fine," Maclean said. "Don't you worry."

"Good night, then," Legs said. "And you look after your-self."

"Good night, Legs," Maclean said. "And you look after yourself too."

Maclean watched him walk off into the shadows, his gait as angular and delicate as the final steps of a soft shoe dancer disappearing into the wings.

Then he turned and set off back down the hill.

Most of the houses he passed were dark, though here and there an upstairs light was still on where someone maybe was lying in bed reading or listening to the far-away stations that came in sometimes late in the evening, even on the dull-eared, asthmatic, old radio at Drusilla's. Once he heard, from far off on another street, the sound of someone playing something complicated and sad on a piano. Once from a darkened house close by, the sound of a woman laughing.

After a quarter of an hour's walk, slow and steady, he came to the Court House with its twin memorials of the Great War on the lawn out front—the gray German field gun on its square concrete platform and on the other side of the lawn, the cenotaph with its gray-granite soldier standing at attention on his pedestal, gun and soldier both spectral in the moonlight.

He stopped on the sidewalk in front of the gun and looked up at it. In front of the shield on either side of the barrel were narrow metal seats with foot rests where two of the gunners could sit when the gun was being towed, although the seats must, he thought, have been damned hard on the ass.

He looked around. The street was deserted, the houses all

dark. He walked up the slope of the lawn, mounted the concrete platform, and heaved himself up onto one of the seats on the gun. It was damned hard on the ass, but maybe they folded up their greatcoats and used them as cushions.

He wondered where the gun had been captured and imagined the gunners lying dead around it, along some road maybe where the shells had caught them, or in a field scythed clean by a machine gun, or in the bottom of a gun pit where the gas had collected.

It was too bad about the McIntyre boy who wouldn't be coming home, as some people so delicately put it, stepping with averted gaze around the reality of what would have happened. But maybe none of them had ever come home. Maybe only their ghosts had come home, as some poet had said. Maybe one way or another, quick or slow, they had all died of their wounds. And maybe that wasn't so different, after all, from the way life happened for everybody. Maybe the whole thing was a war, leaving behind its trail of dead and wounded, its trail of sad ghosts haunting the ruins of their lives. In his kind of war, it had happened a lot quicker than in what they call peace, condensing into a few months what otherwise took decades, but peace or war, it happened all the same.

He thought of Mrs. Fraser who had no doubt once loved and begotten in joy, now lying in her bed, looking up at the ceiling, waiting for death, of Miss Audrey Sweet who had once loved, as the saying went, not wisely but too well, of Alice who had once recited Wordsworth to Harry Noles, of Miss Mazerole who had once seen Paris, of Legs who had once danced and played the banjo, of Ellie who had once sung "Rock of Ages," of Henry, having fled his unprofitable farm, sitting out at night on the rock with his telescope studying the stars and wondering what the hell it was all about.

And, of course, always and everywhere, high up and low down, there were the bastards, the ones you could only get away from by sneaking off for an hour or two to some hidden, little corner like Ellie's place. That's the way it always had been and that's the way it always would be. So fuck it.

He took out the pony with the last of the rum, unscrewed the cap, and took a sip, rolling the rum around in his mouth, savouring the warm sweetness those far-away, tropical islands had imbued it with. Past the lighthouse, past the nunbuoy, past the crimson, rising sun.

He placed the bottle carefully in the corner of the seat behind him and sat on, letting the warmth spread. He could have gone to sleep sitting there, and every couple of minutes, he told himself he had better get up and go before he did fall asleep. And before someone saw him and called the police and had him thrown in the jug because it wasn't considered good for the well-being of society that a man with a bottle should be sitting on an old field gun thinking about life in the middle of the night.

After another quarter of an hour, he roused himself. He unscrewed the cap of his bottle and drank the last of the rum. He let it find its way and when it had, climbed sleepily down off the gun, the bottle still in one hand, the cap in the other. He studied them carefully, then screwed the cap back on the bottle and popped it into the barrel of the gun.

He picked his way across the lawn to the cenotaph and walked around it twice, very slowly, looking at the long columns of names on the black tablets. He knew where every name was of the boys who had been his pals. Robert Cronk. Charles Simpson. Henry Noles. William Sperry. Frank Gallagher. Daniel McGrath. Ebenezer Watson. Edward McDade. Here. Here. Here. All present and accounted for.

He ran his fingers over the engraved names of Bob and Harry like a man reading braile.

They shall not grow old, the dignitaries at Remembrance Day were fond of intoning, as we that are left grow old. Age shall not weary them nor the years condemn. And so forth.

At the foot of the steps up to the cenotaph, he turned and waved a sloppy, limp-wristed good night to the soldier on top, then set off on the last leg of his walk home.

Main Street was deserted, not a car, not a soul anywhere. A streetlight hung on a metal cable over the intersection where the Salvation Army band had played and the policeman had stood directing traffic. Two more lights on poles stood on either side of the square at the bottom of the street making pools of light in which floated the litter cast away by the Saturday night crowds.

Just below the post office, he stepped off the curb onto the street, stumbled a little, righted himself, and began to march, first close to the sidewalk, then out and straight down the middle, his arms swinging wider and wider arcs as he passed the store windows and the darkened displays. Cascades of apples and new potatoes flowing out of artfully tipped baskets. A smooth slope of green where the jewels of Marathon MacClewan had been spread. A poster with a picture of Wilf Carter in a white ten-gallon hat smiling toothily above a pile of records. Whole roomfuls of furniture. Gatherings of immaculately dressed dummies, important gents in double-breasted suits, elegant ladies in their autumn dresses, staring glassily at each other, sightless and serene.

He glanced at them indifferently as he passed. He was elsewhere now. Slowly out of the great gulf of the past, the boys took shape around him. Bob, Frank, and Harry. Dan. Bill. Charlie. All just the way they had been before the bad things started to happen, swinging along in the close-packed, khaki lines of the old battalion, marching at ease, their rifles slung on their shoulders, the peaked caps tipped back, the sun streaming down, the band playing.

As he approached the square, he began to hum to himself in strict march time and then to sing.

Pack up your troubles in your old kit bag
And smile, smile, smile,
While you've a lucifer to light your fag,
Smile, boys, that's the style.

In an upstairs window above a store, a large man in his undershirt with his braces hanging loose stared down at him, then slowly drew down the blind.

Allan Donaldson was born in Taber, Alberta, but grew up in Woodstock, New Brunswick, shiretown of a county that was settled overwhelmingly by Irish and Scots, among whom were ancestors going back to the early nineteenth century. As a child, he became well acquainted with the street life of the town. In his teens, he had summer jobs wheeling cement, tamping ties and laying steel on the railway, working on a rock crusher and an asphalt plant, and operating a jack-hammer. On scholarships, he studied English literature at the University of New Brunswick and the University of London, and he spent a teaching career in the English Department at the University of New Brunswick. He is the author of a book of short stories, *Paradise Siding*, published by Goose Lane.

A Note On The Type

This book was set in Adobe Caslon Pro. In 1722, William Caslon released the first of his typefaces. They were based on Dutch forms of the 17th century, which were popular in England at the time. Due to their functionality, Caslon's typefaces quickly spread throughout the western world. Printer Benjamin Franklin used the typeface extensively. In her work with Adobe, American type designer Carol Twombly re-drew and merged lettertypes from documents printed by William Caslon, and added additional ligatures and support for other European languages. Twombly was the first woman to receive the Charles Peignot award for outstanding contribution to typography.